THE DEMON KING'S COOK

EverEri

DEDICATION

For those who have been made to feel you don't deserve love because of your looks, the ones who love you see your true beauty. You deserve to be loved just as much as everyone else.

Content Warning

The content in this book may not be suitable for everyone. Please be aware that this book contains the following:

Explicit Sex Scenes
Mild violence
DP
Anal

If any of this concerns you, then this book may not be for you.

Chapter 1

It was inspection day, and Viridian, the demon in charge of making sure everything was in order at the estate, had been in a mood for weeks. Not that he was ever friendly.

I wasn't afraid of the master of the demon king's estate like so many others were. He made me nervous, knowing he could squash me like a bug, but he had never harmed anyone who had come to Ethlow for refuge. The worst he did was send daggers with his eyes, scowl, or the occasional lash from his tongue. No physical damage ever occurred. Emotional damage was a different story.

As long as the residents followed the three main rules of the house, we were allowed to stay.

1. Do Your Work.

2. Don't go out after dark.

3. Stay away from the demon king.

Only, the third rule didn't seem to matter anymore, not with Nyri dating the king. Viridian had grown more tense as my human friend shared a bed with the demon king. It was as if the master of the house was waiting for the ramifications of a human and demon dating. A lot of us were, but Nyri had never looked happier.

She didn't see what her dating the demon king did to the rest of us. The kitchen had never looked better, but Viridian had gotten harsher with his weekly inspections. He would see something I had missed, and even though I wasn't the one in charge of the kitchen, I was the one who'd take the fall for it. Cibil was the head chef, but the gnome had long reached their prime. They were sweet, but the old gnome spent the majority of their kitchen shift napping instead of working.

Deep breaths. Everything in the kitchen was sparkling. Everything was going to be okay. The strict demon would arrive at any moment for his weekly inspection.

"Wow. I don't think I have ever seen anything so clean before." Reamann's echoed from behind me, making me yelp.

I glared at the demon guard. He picked the worst time to swing by the kitchen and bother me—not that it was hard for him to do. I had never met someone with such a voracious appetite. He stopped by the kitchen at all hours of the day. He asked for snacks and second lunch—something I could never get away with without gaining more weight. I didn't look like most of the other residents of my size, but Reamann was rippling with muscles. He was one of the larger and more in shape guardsmen I had seen. It explained his inhuman appetite—so did his demonic nature—but that didn't make it less annoying.

"Not now, Reamann. I'm busy." I turned my back on the orange-haired fiend, looking for anything I could clean. A small crumb near the stove had tried to escape, but I was determined to receive a perfect inspection.

"Aw, come on, Kina. There's no one in the mess hall right now. Can't you make me one of your famous fish rolls?" Reamann asked for seafood the most. I hadn't decided if that was his way of messing with me due to my mermaid genes, or if he was completely oblivious to the fact that asking a mermaid to constantly make seafood was like asking a human to cook her dog.

I placed my hand on my hip, intensifying my glare. "No one is here because Master Viridian is supposed to arrive at any moment, and everyone else is smart enough to stay clear of him. So no, I can't make you a fish roll right now."

Reamann pinched his lips together, looking down at the counter with his big, red eyes. Despite his large size and demonic nature, he looked like a puppy. My irritation cracked under his gaze. I was weak.

I rolled my eyes, my defenses breaking. "I will make you a fish roll after Master Viridian finishes his inspection, so stop giving me that sad look."

Reamann's entire face brightened at the mention of food. "You're the best. I'm starving." If I hadn't known better, I would've guessed the demon guard was manipulating me, but he didn't seem to have a thought behind those two red eyes of his.

"You were here for lunch two hours ago." I couldn't imagine how he ate as much as he did while maintaining practically no fat on his body. I ate a third of what he did, and my stomach and ass suffered for it.

"Exactly. It's time for second lunch." Reamann rubbed his belly through his black leather armor.

I shook my head. I gave into his whims too easily. It was hard not to when pure joy filled his face whenever he ate my food. No one else got that much pleasure from eating something I had made.

"Now get out of here." I waved my hands, shooing Reamann away.

"I hope you don't talk to all the residents like that," Viridian said from behind me.

My entire body tensed. Viridian moved through the shadows, making his appearance silent and sudden. "Sorry, Master Viridian. I didn't see you there."

Reamann chuckled, but when Viridian's teal eyes settled on the guard, he straightened his back, hardening his features to look serious. "I should get back to duty."

"Yes, you should," Viridian said. He didn't bother scolding Reamann. He didn't have to. A single look from the demon sent the guardsman running.

Viridian's bat-winged horns fluttered as he turned back to the kitchen. One hand rested on his torso while the other was folded behind his back. He wore a suit with intricate stitching, and white gloves that covered the sharp, black nails beneath. The only color in the demon's outfit belonged to the teal ruffles around his neck, so dark they were almost black, matching the color of his hair. His teal eyes simmered with power.

He searched the kitchen for any signs of imperfection, and I moved out of his way, grateful I had sent the rest of the staff away, not wanting them to face the scrutiny from the master of the house. After five years, I had learned how to deal with the demon, but others weren't used to the intensity of the master of the house.

Viridian took a few steps, scanning everything. I held my breath, waiting for him to find the one thing I had missed. He said nothing, leaving me on edge. He stopped at the sink and picked up something I couldn't see with two fingers. He held it to the light, his lips twitching.

"You missed a crumb, Aukina."

My heart pounded against my ribs, desperate to be free of the situation. If Reamann hadn't interrupted me, I would've found the crumb. Everything would've been perfect. "It's only one." I had made a mistake the moment I spoke.

Viridian's eyes narrowed. "A crumb could lead to vermin invading the kitchen. If they invade the kitchen, they will spread to the rest of the estate, and then everyone will have to deal with rodents. I *hate* rats."

"It won't happen again." I gritted my teeth, knowing arguing with the demon would only make the situation worse.

Black smoke erupted from his fingertips, eviscerating the crumb. "See to it that it doesn't, because if I see a single rat, I will know exactly who to blame." He stepped into the shadows, and his body molded into them, making him disappear in a split second.

I collapsed against the counter, finally able to breathe again. The air grew thick whenever Viridian showed up. I wasn't sure if it was from my fear or from the demon's magic poisoning the air. It didn't matter. He was gone after giving a mild scolding. It was better than last time. I pressed my hand against my chest, waiting for my heart to slow. I was safe from judgment for another week.

"Viridian gives me the chills." Reamann leaned against the counter that separated me from the mess hall.

"If he heard you calling him anything other than 'master,' you'd get in trouble." I forced myself to stand up straight, not wanting Reamann to see the stress attacking my body. He dealt with scarier enemies than crumbs as part of the guardsmen.

Reamann pressed his elbows on the counter, leaning forward. "It was just a crumb. He doesn't need to be so harsh. You keep this place running better than Cibil ever did."

"Don't say that." I grabbed several ingredients from the fridge, intent on keeping my promise to make Reamann his fish rolls. "She's a legend. She has run the kitchen for longer than most residents have been here—longer than I've been alive." I was a baby at twenty-eight years in the mermaid realm. Most mermaids lived to at least three centuries, but that was nothing compared to the immortals that lived in Ethlow.

"She never seasoned food like you do, and she never made seafood. When you showed up, the food became more than edible. It was something to look forward to, especially knowing you were in the kitchen." Reamann had been at Ethlow when I arrived at the demon king's estate, but I didn't know how long he had been there. He was a lesser demon, but that was the extent of what I knew besides his favorite foods. I didn't know his age or what kind of demonic powers he possessed. I had never asked.

"What's your obsession with seafood?" I wrinkled my nose as I cut the fish into thin slices. The thought of eating my fellow sea dwellers felt wrong. I stuck to plants with the occasional land animal. Most mermaids only ate plants, because that was what we grew up with in the sea. My time on the Nescen Islands had made me develop a taste for beef, which was rare for merfolk. I was one of the few that dared to step out of the sea.

"It's delicious. If I could eat it for every meal, I would." He licked his lips.

I hid my grimace. He was an idiot. A big, muscular idiot who always bothered me at the worst moments.

I finished my final touches on the fish roll, cutting it into bite-sized pieces. Reamann's eyes lit up with delight as I pushed the plate towards him. I wondered what it was like to get as excited about eating as he did. It was hard to truly delight in my food when I was worried about how much of it would go straight to my oversized hips.

"I think it would do you good to get away from Ethlow for a bit," Reamann said after devouring half of his meal with a few bites. "Maybe we could—"

"Aukina!" Wistari, one of the kitchen helpers, ran into the room. She was a small thing, an elven girl who hadn't reached full maturity. Her blonde hair flew behind her, down to her lower spine. "Ovid is halfway down the path and will be here soon."

My face heated at the mention of the merchant. "Already? He wasn't supposed to be here until tomorrow." Ovid delivered the weekly supplies to the kitchen, providing us with everything he could from the list I provided each week. It was the highlight of my week, but I wasn't ready. I hadn't worn my most flattering dress or put a touch of makeup on my eyes. Today was supposed to be about Viridian's inspection. Ovid wasn't supposed to arrive until tomorrow.

"Hurry. He's almost here." Wistari tugged at my arm.

I glanced back at Reamann, who had stopped eating. "I'll see you later."

The guard didn't have a chance to respond as I hurried out of the room, combing my fingers through my hair. The wheels of the rickety wagon clattered closer as I stepped outside. Ovid used the back entrance of the demon king's estate. Viridian didn't like supplies being lugged through the front entrance, saying it was gaudy, and the demon king was above that. After meeting the demon king, I was convinced it was Viridian's personal preference.

I smoothed my blue dress down to make myself look more presentable. It wasn't my favorite yellow dress that brought the flecks of gold out of my dark brown eyes, but it looked nice against my darker skin. I waved to Ovid as he rounded the corner, biting my lip to stop myself from looking overly excited.

Every week, I told myself I'd confess my feelings for the merchant. Every week I chickened out. I rarely caught the eye of males on land, and the last time I had confessed my feelings, I was rejected, saying I wasn't pretty enough. If that human had known who I was, he wouldn't have rejected me, but that was why I kept my ancestry a secret. I didn't want people to treat me differently because of who gave birth to me.

"Good afternoon, my shimmering Aukina," Ovid said with his thick accent.

My shimmering Aukina. He had never said anything like that to me before. Heat crawled up my neck and into my face. I grabbed my skirt and curtsied. "Hello Ovid." I silently scolded myself for curtsying. I had never done something like that. "I wasn't expecting you until tomorrow."

"I wanted to come early. They say a storm is brewing, and I wanted to make sure my best customer got everything she needed." He gestured to the sky. It was clear, except for a few clouds in the distance, but the weather was finicky during the summer, often bringing sudden storms.

"You are such a gentleman." Ovid made a special trip just for me. It made me want to twirl in grassy fields.

"I do what I can. I managed to get everything you requested. I'm surprised you ordered so much seafood. I thought mermaids don't eat fish." Ovid worked on unloading boxes of supplies.

I tucked my thick, black hair behind my ear. "We don't, but I cook for all the residents." Ovid remembered small things like that. It was one of the reasons I liked him. Not to mention, his half-fae ancestry gave him the looks of a god. His black hair was silky smooth and went past his shoulders. Dark stubble covered his chin, making me wonder what it'd feel like to kiss him.

"Ever the people pleaser," Ovid chuckled. "You should do something for yourself for once."

I opened my mouth, ready to ask him out. It was the perfect time. Ovid had complimented me and made a special trip for me. He liked me. I was sure of it.

Fear stole my voice, and I clamped my mouth shut before he saw me gaping like a guppy. Instead, I watched Ovid unload the last of the boxes, knowing it was another day my feelings for him would stay locked inside. I tried to tell myself it was because I wasn't dressed my best, but it was a lie. A small part of me prayed to Artagatis, the goddess of mermaids, that Ovid would ask me out first, saving me the embarrassment of a rejection.

"Is that it?" I asked when the cart was empty.

Ovid smiled, making my heart swoon. "For now, yes."

"Ah." I wanted to kick myself for my awkwardness. It was easy to talk to most beings, but Ovid made me stumble over my words.

Ovid stroked his white horse, taking his time as if he was delaying leaving. "I've heard some rumors recently that the demon king's estate has a bleeding heart lily growing here." He glanced at me from the side. He was gorgeous from every angle.

"Oh, we do!" Nyri had worked hard to grow the rare flower in the greenhouse. Bleeding heart lilies had a difficult time growing in Kinzlea because of the cold, dry weather, but Nyri had magic that brought life to the flowers. Before that, I hadn't seen the flower since leaving the Hallow Sea. Bleeding heart lilies bloomed with ease on the Nescen Islands where the humidity was high. Nyri had no idea that she had brought a piece of home to Ethlow. "It's stunning."

Ovid turned, leaning against his horse in a way that made his muscles bulge. "I'd love to see it sometime." He licked his lips, drawing my attention to his plump mouth. "Maybe you and I could go together."

All of my prayers to Artagatis had finally paid off. "I'd love to," I squeaked.

Ovid smirked. "Next time then, my lustrous fish."

I watched him walk away, barely feeling my body. After all of these years, Ovid had finally asked *me* out. It was a dream, one that made my body feel lighter than it ever had on land.

Only once the merchant was out of sight did I pick up a box of supplies to put it away. I turned around, but the box was plucked out of my arms.

"That guy is a tool," Reamann muttered, holding the crate with ease.

I yelped, not expecting the guard to be right there. I placed my hand on my chest. "Holy Mackerel. Don't sneak up on me like that."

Reamann pressed his lips into a thin line. The joy that had been on his face earlier was nowhere to be found. "He didn't bother to help you bring this stuff into his kitchen."

"That's because I can do it myself, and he's busy. I'm not his only customer." I tried to take the box from Reamann, but he twisted away from me.

"I don't like him." The guard walked towards the kitchen.

I quickly grabbed another box and rushed to catch up with him, ignoring the ache in my lungs. I didn't want him to think I was weak. "Good thing it doesn't matter if you like him. Because I do."

Reamann's face tightened, but he didn't say anything. I didn't understand what his problem was, but it didn't matter. Ovid asked me out, and in a week, we'd have our first date.

Chapter 2

"But did he actually use the words, 'Will you go out with me?'" Satella asked. She was the demon king's healer, and she had been my longest friend at Ethlow. She pushed her short, curly hair out of the way, revealing her undercut. Her nails were decorated with flowers in honor of the summer. She was always changing the design of her nails.

Nyri and Satella sat in the abandoned courtyard where the three of us made a point to have dinner together daily. Even with Nyri dating the demon king—something I still struggled to wrap my mind around—she carved out the pre-dinner time with us. It was easier for me to eat dinner before the rush.

"He asked me to go see the bleeding heart lily with him," I said between bites.

Nyri munched on her food, pursing her lips. "That could be a date, depending." Her light brown hair was tied back to keep it from touching her food.

"It could be something more." Satella wiggled her eyebrows. She was stretched out on the ground with her hands resting on her stomach, letting the sun warm her skin. I never understood her. She was a vampire, which meant the sun weakened her, but she loved it anyway. I preferred the shadows, where it was cooler. My body ran warm, since it was used to the icy sea, so the summer sun made me feel like I was a lobster in boiling water.

"What do you mean by more?" I asked. I had a feeling I knew where Satella was going with this, but the thought of saying it out loud made me blush. It had been too long since I had been intimate with someone, and I had never had sex in my human form. It was different with legs.

"Think about what Zathrian and Nyri used to sneak off to do in the greenhouse," Satella said. "They probably still do."

Nyri bit her lip, but she was unable to hide her smile. She glowed with happiness since she and the demon king came out with their relationship. It made me nervous knowing how the demon king's last relationship ended, but I didn't say anything. My friend was happy. That was what mattered most.

"We don't," Nyri quickly said. Neither of us believed her.

"Doesn't mean that isn't what the lover boy merchant is planning." Satella closed her eyes, basking like a sea turtle on a chilly winter day.

"Ovid isn't like that," I said. He seemed like the guy who would take his time making a woman swoon. He took years to ask me out, because he wanted to get to know me. He didn't ask me to go to the greenhouse for a hookup.

"If you want, I can make sure no one goes into the greenhouse when you and Ovid go," Nyri said. "That way you guys have some privacy, and you can get to know him properly." She winked, implying something more. Her offer sounded innocent, but the things she did with the demon king said otherwise. Innocent was the last word I'd use to describe her.

I almost declined out of nerves, but I planned on confessing my feelings to Ovid. I knew myself well enough to know I'd chicken out if anyone else was around. "That'd be great, actually."

"Consider it done," Nyri said." It's going to be so romantic. The bleeding heart lily is looking better than ever. I still can't believe I made it grow on this dry land." Nyri glowed as she talked about her flower. It was her prized possession, and it gave her purpose. The entire greenhouse did.

"The flower is really beautiful," Satella agreed.

It had been awhile since I had gone to see the flower. The thought of going with Ovid made my heart race.

Nyri stood, collecting her empty tray. "I should get going. Zath is waiting for me." She said her goodbyes, leaving Satella and me alone.

The vampire sat up slowly. "It's a little sickening how in love she is, isn't it?"

I chuckled. "A little bit. I'm more jealous that she was only here for a few weeks before she got her happy ending."

"It's not a happy ending," Satella said. "It's a happy beginning, and if things go well with Ovid, maybe you'll get the next happy beginning."

I didn't see Reamann once the next day. After dinner, I grew worried. He had only skipped one meal before, so him skipping an entire day of eating pulled my attention. I felt guilty, wondering if it was because of me. When we parted after Ovid's delivery, the guard was acting weird. I was worried I had said something to upset him.

I walked to the barracks with leftovers from dinner packed inside. The sound of metal clanging filled my ears. In the five years I had been at Ethlow, I had only visited the barracks a few times. I didn't belong in a place like that, so I avoided it when possible. I had never fought or trained for anything other than proper etiquette.

Heavy grunts replaced the ringing metal. The smell of sweat and dirt filled the air. Reamann stood in the middle of the room with a blond fae wrapped around his neck. His face turned red as oxygen was cut off to his lungs. I pressed the container of food against my chest as I watched, trying to stave off my concerns. The guards were training. There was nothing to worry about.

Reamann bent his knees and leaned forward, flipping the other guy over him. The blond hit the ground with a thud, making me squeak. He didn't try to get up, his bare chest heaving up and down. Reamann stood over him, also not wearing a shirt. His pecs and abs glistened with sweat. He wiped his forehead, and then offered his hand out to the other guard.

"You're getting better, Iolas," Reamann said. He patted the man on the back.

The blond nudged him in the ribs, gesturing to me. Reamann's red eyes snapped over to mine, and my heart raced. I didn't know why I went to the barracks. Reamann and I weren't close friends. We didn't hang out outside the kitchen, but the thought of him being mad at me was unbearable.

I waited for the orange-haired guard to smile at me like he always did, but his face was unreadable. He was definitely mad at me. He held up his pointer finger, gesturing for me to give him a moment. I shifted my weight back and forth, looking at the weapons displayed on the walls. If the demon king's estate ever came under siege, the guardsmen were ready to defend the place. It had been peaceful in the five years I had been at Ethlow, but there had been a time that wasn't the case.

A millenia ago, the five demon rulers were at war, fighting to become the ruler of all. The problem was the five demons held immense power that could destroy everything. The war raged on for longer than it should've, not one demon strong enough to best another. Eventually, a truce was called.

"Sorry, I took so long." Reamann wore a clean shirt, but his hair was plastered with sweat.

"It's not a problem." I lifted the box of food. "You hadn't come to the kitchen today, so I was a little worried. I thought I'd bring you leftovers."

Reamann's face lit up, any lingering anger disappearing. "You noticed I wasn't there today?"

I punched him in the arm but was quickly surprised by the solid muscle my knuckles were met with. I stopped myself from wincing. "How could I not notice? You're like a two-tailed fish when it comes to food. You never miss a meal. I thought you might have been sick."

"I was busy." Reamann scratched the back of his head. "Do you want to go for a walk? A pretty lady like you shouldn't be surrounded by this much sweat."

The laugh that came out of my mouth was sharper than usual, my nerves making it sound fake. "Do you think a little sweat would bother me? When you work in a hot kitchen all day, you sweat. A lot. I'm sure you've noticed."

"I thought you were glowing."

I shook my head. "Beaded jellyfish glow. Mermaids on land sweat." Reamann was sweet, but he was completely oblivious.

Reamann led the way out of the building, and I followed. The soft breeze countered the stuffiness of the training area, making me grateful for his suggestion.

He stopped under the shade of a tree. "So, what's for dinner?"

I handed him the box. "Fried fish tartar."

Reamann practically drooled as he opened the box. With the first bite, he let out a long, satisfied hum. The weight on my chest lightened, seeing him delight in my food. "This is incredible," he said with his second bite already in his mouth.

"Good. I was worried you were mad at me when you didn't show up today." I twisted the ends of my black hair, looking at the ground.

Reamann swallowed, already halfway through the meal. "I was switched to the night shift, so I didn't have time to swing by like usual. This is technically my breakfast." He hesitated, looking away. "If I'm honest, I was thrown off when I found out you liked the merchant. I wasn't aware you liked anyone."

It took a moment for me to form a response. I hadn't talked to many people about my crush, because it was embarrassing to pine over someone who didn't feel the same.

"I know it's not my business, but I don't get a good vibe from that merchant," Reamann continued when I didn't say anything. "I want you to be careful. That's all."

"There's nothing for you to worry about. Ovid is a good guy." I bit back the smile that wanted to creep onto my face as I thought about seeing Ovid next week.

"I'm going to worry about you. I don't want any creeps pulling you down. You deserve better." The judgment in his voice made my chest twinge.

"It's not like there are males lining up at my door, asking me out on a date. I'm not exactly attractive. Ovid is a good guy, but you're right. It's not any of your business. We're going to see the bleeding heart lily next time he comes around, and I'm going to confess my feelings to him." I clamped my lips shut, unsure of why I told Reamann all of that. I didn't need to defend myself to the guard.

"You're blinded by his good looks. I'm telling you he's bad news. My gut is never wrong about these things."

"Your gut is an endless whirlpool of hunger," I snapped. "You don't know Ovid, and you don't know what's good for me, so keep your opinions to yourself." I stormed off, more irritated with Reamann than I had been yesterday.

The rain was relentless for the next several days. I pressed my cheek against the wooden table, staring at the weather I usually considered beautiful, but I couldn't leave the building with the heavy rain. I turned into my mermaid form if my body got too wet. I loved the rain. It made the air more humid, but today the heavy drops reminded me of home.

I hadn't spoken to my mother and father since the day I left, renouncing my heritage in the process. It had been over five years since that fateful day. Only a few more months, and it'd be a full six years. Most days, I didn't miss my family. They had been suffocating with a hundred responsibilities they shoved onto my shoulders. They hated any time I spent on the Nescen Islands. The day they forbade me to go on land, I left, knowing the future they had planned wasn't for me.

I never regretted leaving, but for the first time in a long time, the rain made me miss the sea. I missed the freedom of a tail, something I hadn't allowed myself to indulge in since leaving. I left behind my family and my responsibilities, and I refused to think about the guilt that sat in the pit of my stomach.

"Oof. That argument with Reamann did a number on you." Satella slid onto the bench on the other side of the table, holding a bowl of soup.

"I don't know what you're talking about," I said. I tried not to think about Reamann and his stupid opinion. He didn't know Ovid like I did.

"I have never seen you this depressed when it rains. Usually you're bouncing off the walls, saying how much you love the rain." Satella sipped her soup. She didn't need regular food for sustenance. Her main source of nutrients came from blood. She liked eating soup for the taste.

"I'm worried that the rain won't let up in time for my date with Ovid." I peeled my cheek off the table.

Satella's eyebrows were slightly raised as she gave me a knowing look. "Reamann hasn't shown up since the day you came back in a huff."

"He's on night duty. That's all." Deep down, I knew that wasn't the only reason the orange-haired demon hadn't been to the mess hall.

"And it's a coincidence that you've been in a foul mood since he stopped coming around." Satella laid the sarcasm on thickly, which didn't help my irritation.

"Yes. It's good that Reamann hasn't been around. I don't need him judging my choices. Who does he think he is, telling me he doesn't think Ovid is a good guy?" I had replayed that conversation over a thousand times. Reamann usually acted like sunshine, so his grumpiness didn't sit well.

Satella picked up her bowl, slurping the last of her soup. "Sounds like he's jealous."

"Jealous? Of what?" Reamann had no reason to be jealous. He was attractive and nice. Everyone loved him.

"Of Ovid. I think he likes you." The vampire winked at me.

My mouth fell open, and Satella chuckled. She walked away before I could form a response. There was no way the demon guard thought of me like that.

Chapter 3

Artagatis was watching over me. The clouds parted, and the sun came out the day Ovid was supposed to come back. I tried to focus on prepping the meals for the day, but it was difficult to focus knowing the merchant would arrive at any moment. When Wistari came running, I was moving before she said a word. I held up the skirts of my favorite yellow dress as I ran. The wheels of the cart clunked against the stone path, and I slowed my pace, composing myself like a perfect lady.

Ovid guided his horse to the usual spot. His bright smile met mine. He had never looked at me with so much joy before, and it set my pulse racing. After years of pining, it was finally happening. I didn't know what had changed in Ovid's heart. Maybe he simply found the courage to ask me out, the same courage I had been searching for ever since his blue eyes met mine.

Ovid hopped off his cart and flipped his hair. He looked stunning, making it difficult to find my words. I tucked a piece of hair behind my ear, my smile burning my cheeks.

"Good morning," I said, my voice an octave higher than intended.

"Good morning, my delicate oyster fish," Ovid sang.

I stopped myself from twitching at the pet name. Oyster fish weren't known for their beauty, but Ovid didn't mean anything by it. Plus, with his accent, he made everything sound beautiful.

"Were the roads kind to you?" I asked.

"Very. It is a miracle the sun decided to come out on the day I was meant to come to Ethlow. It is as if the gods and goddesses have blessed me." He placed his hands on his hips and looked up at the sky.

"I was thinking the same thing." I pulled at my skirts, wanting to make sure they looked perfect. "I was thinking we could see the bleeding heart lily first and then unload everything?" I was eager to confess my feelings to the merchant before I lost my fleeting courage.

The intensity in Ovid's eyes made my heart skip. "A wonderful idea."

I hesitated, hoping he'd offer me his arm to walk alongside him. When he didn't, I cleared my throat. "It's this way."

The walk to the greenhouse was spent in silence. I didn't know what to say to Ovid, unable to think about anything other than the confession I had practiced repeatedly over the past week.

When we reached the glass building, Ovid let out a long whistle. "I haven't seen a greenhouse like this in all of Kinzlea. It is like a diamond sparkling in the rays of the sun."

"Nyri and the king did an incredible job cleaning it up. It was abandoned for decades before they decided to revive it." I opened the door to the greenhouse, and Ovid walked past me. I quickly caught up with him, slowing my pace once I was by his side.

The merchant didn't stop until he stood directly in front of the bleeding heart lily. It was in the center of the greenhouse and easy to see from the entrance. Gold ropes blocked off the space around the flower to stop visitors from reaching out and touching the delicate leaves. Ovid inched closer, the rope pulling against his torso. I lifted my hand, wanting to tell him to take a step back, but I was afraid to offend him.

"Aine," Ovid muttered under his breath. "It is more beautiful than anything I have ever seen. No wonder the flower is worth buckets of gold."

The white flower petals opened wide, taking in the sun, but that wasn't the most mesmerizing part of the flower. Red tendrils flowed from the center, like blood pouring from a heart. It was the only flower I had seen that looked as if it was moving when there wasn't a breeze.

"Many think the white bleeding heart lily is the only strain of the flower," I said, thinking about the years I spent on the Nescen Islands, where everything was decorated after the remarkable flower. "But there is a rare mutation with purple leaves and gold tendrils. I have only seen it once, but nothing has ever compared to that experience."

"Purple?" Ovid repeated, not tearing his eyes away from the flower.

"Some people think the purple petals are a myth, but that's because an ice storm destroyed the only known purple variant. Few have seen it, but there is an ancient myth that when a bleeding heart lily witnesses true love, their leaves turn purple, and the blood turns gold." I smiled as I thought about the stories the people of the Nescen Islands used to tell me. I loved their stories.

"That is utter nonsense," Ovid said. "True love doesn't exist."

I furrowed my eyebrows as I looked at the merchant. I must've misheard him. "Surely, you can't mean that."

Ovid clasped his hands behind his back, not bothering to look at me as he spoke. "I do. People think they're in love, but it's a fool's game. It's mother nature's way of tricking the people of the land to repopulate, but true love doesn't exist. True love is loving someone more than anything else in the world. People simply mistake lust for love. That is why I prefer material objects."

I blinked slowly, unsure of how to respond. I had been sure Ovid liked me, but his words made me question that. "Why did you ask me to join you here?" Part of me didn't want to know the answer, afraid it wasn't what I wanted to hear.

Ovid looked at me for the first time, studying my face carefully. "You didn't think I was asking you out, did you?"

My chest clenched. "I thought this was a date." The admission made me feel like a foolish girl for making an assumption.

Ovid's sharp laugh ripped through my heart. "I could never ask out someone like..." He looked me up and down. "Like you. I prefer my women slender. Not ones who like to eat the kitchen staff with their meals."

The world around me felt like it was cracking, and I struggled to find my breath. It wasn't the first time I had heard something like that, but I had thought Ovid was different. "Why did you ask me here?" I repeated.

"Because I wanted to see the bleeding heart lily, and I couldn't do that without you."

"So you used me?"

Ovid rolled his eyes. "Don't be so dramatic. You wanted to come here with me."

"When I thought you liked me," I snapped, shocking myself. I rarely spoke like that to anyone, but my heart was crumbling. I spent years pining for a man who thought so little of me.

"No one could like a whale like you. You should accept that now." Ovid's eyes were cold and distant. I should've known better. Land dwellers cared about body shape. In the sea, it was different. We loved everyone for who they were, inside and out. Tall, short, skinny, fat, blue scales, gray scales. It didn't matter as much as a merfolk's heart.

"Get out." I pointed at the door, my hand shaking. I used to think myself beautiful, but males like Ovid had changed the image I saw in the mirror, one comment at a time.

Ovid's face twisted with confusion, as if he hadn't expected me to stand up for myself. "I will leave when I'm ready. You don't own this place. You're simply a cook. Nothing more. You probably can't even cook that well."

Something snapped inside of me, and I shoved Ovid's chest. "I said get out!"

Ovid stumbled backwards. He stared at me with a blank face. Then he rushed forward, grabbing my arms. "How dare you lay your hands on me."

I stomped on his foot and then slammed my leg between his. He groaned and shoved me hard. I lost balance, hitting my face on a metal table. I touched my forehead and felt something warm and sticky.

"You're not worth this," Ovid said before storming off.

I didn't follow him. I didn't move, a wave of numbness washing over me. It was one thing for Ovid to not like me back, but I had thought highly of him. I had defended him to Reamann and my friends, but the guard had been right. Ovid was sea scum, and I was the girl foolish enough to fall for him.

The supplies Ovid had brought for the week were dumped all over the ground. Several boxes were damaged, and the contents sat on the dirt. My head was foggy, but I wasn't sure if it was from the way Ovid had spoken to me, or if it was from the cut on my head. I knew I should've gone to Satella right away to get checked out, but some of the supplies Ovid brought needed to be put in the ice box before it spoiled.

I crouched down to grab the first box of supplies. Footsteps crunched towards me, and I froze. I didn't know who it was, but I didn't want them to see the blood on my dress where I had used it to slow the bleeding from the cut on my forehead. They'd ask questions about things I didn't want to answer. I wanted to forget about Ovid and the greenhouse.

I waited, hoping whoever it was passed by on their way to somewhere else. The footsteps stopped, and I held my breath. Shuffling sounds filled the air, pulling my attention. I peeked over my shoulder and saw burning, orange hair as Reamann picked up a large crate.

I stood a little too quickly, making my head spin. I kept my back turned to Reamann. He was the last person I wanted to see.

"What are you doing here?" I asked, the bite in my voice gone.

"Helping you put the supplies away. What else?" Reamann's voice was sharp, which was unlike him.

"Why? I'm sure you're not a big fan of me right now." I felt Reamann staring at my back, but I refused to turn around. I had to find a way to get him to leave before he saw the blood.

"Whether or not I'm mad at you doesn't change the fact that you deserve help bringing the supplies in—something that merchant should be doing, but apparently he's too lazy to help his customers."

"It's fine. You don't have to help me. I can do this myself. I've done it every week for years. Today isn't any different." I chewed on my inner cheek, hoping he'd leave it alone.

Reamann let out a long sigh. "Look, Aukina, I'm sorry. I know I put my nose in your business when it wasn't my place. You can date whoever you want, and I'll support you. I just... I miss my friend. Can we stop fighting now?"

My lip quivered. I would've preferred Reamann's anger, especially when I was angry at myself.

"Aukina, please. I hate thinking you're mad at me." He set down the box of supplies and stepped closer. When he grabbed my arm, I flinched. "Aukina— What's that?" He grabbed my blood-soaked sleeve.

I slowly turned towards him, keeping my eyes glued to the ground. Tears bubbled in my eyes, but I tried to swallow them. I didn't want to cry in front of Reamann.

Reamann grabbed my chin and forced me to look at him. He took one look and said, "What did he do to you?"

Chapter 4

I tried to pull my arm free, but Reamann didn't budge. His red eyes pierced mine, making it impossible to look away.

"It was an accident." I had no reason to defend Ovid. He was the lowest of sea worms. But defending him felt like defending myself, since I was the ignorant one who fell for him.

Reamann's face tightened as his eyes focused on the cut on my forehead. He loosened his grip, but he didn't let go. I didn't try to pull away again.

"You've been crying."

I took a haggard breath. I wanted to tell Reamann everything, but he had been right about Ovid. It wasn't easy to admit. I pulled back, shame filling my lungs. I couldn't look him in the eyes as I admitted what I wished I could have kept secret. "I should've listened to you. You warned me that Ovid was bad news, but I didn't believe you. I wanted you to be wrong."

Reamann was silent for several seconds, and it was suffocating. I dug my heels into the ground, prepared for him to rub it in that he was right. "I'm sorry."

My gaze snapped to his face. His lips were pressed together. He didn't look smug. He looked genuinely upset. "You are?"

"I... I wish I wasn't right. I don't know what he said or did, but he made you cry. You deserve someone better than that, and I'm sorry the person you liked wasn't better."

My throat tightened, and tears bubbled up, taking over my eyes. I didn't want Reamann to see me cry, so I looked up, forcing the tears to stay back, barely keeping them at bay. "Yeah, well, it's my own fault. I should've known."

"It's not your fault." The kindness in Reamann's voice felt undeserved after the way I had treated him. "It's hard to see what people are really like."

I shrugged, knowing I had been blinded by Ovid's good looks and charming accent. "But if I had listened to you—"

"Don't worry about that." Reamann gave me one of his brilliant smiles. "Right now, we need to get you to Satella, so she can check out the injury on your head."

Reamann wasn't interested in making me feel worse about what happened. Instead, he worried about me and smiled brightly, as if he was trying to improve my mood. He had always been around, but I brushed him off as annoying, because he created extra work for me. Maybe I had been wrong about him.

"I have to get this stuff into the ice box before it spoils." I motioned towards the piles of crates. The broken ones would make the process take nearly twice as long to gather everything.

"You go get checked out, and I'll take care of this stuff." Reamann picked up two crates with ease. I struggled to move one.

"It'd go faster if I helped." I appreciated his offer, but I didn't want him to do my work for me.

Reamann shifted the weight in his hands to get a better grip. "It'd make me feel better if you got checked out now. Don't worry. I know where the stuff goes, and if I need help, I'll ask Wistari."

I was hesitant, but the last time I ignored his advice, I ended up with a broken heart. I let out a sigh. "Fine, but if you need help with anything, call for me."

"I've got this," Reamann said. "Go." He walked towards the kitchen, not bothering to wait for me to argue.

My shoulders slumped, defeat washing over me. Reamann wasn't the only one who'd have questions for me.

I knocked on Satella's door.

"Come in."

I rolled my neck, steeling my nerves to face my friend. I opened the door and looked around the healer's room. Satella sat hunched over her work bench. She rubbed a piece of framed glass with a cloth. When she was done, she held it up.

"Isn't it beautiful?" she cooed. "It arrived this morning. I've been waiting three years for the sapphire crested bee queen to die. I think I'm going to name her Azurite."

Inside the frame, there were several blue bees pinned to a board, displaying their opalescent bodies. The queen bee was the largest and set in the center with twelve bees surrounding her. The sapphire color of the bugs glimmered, even in the soft light of the vampire's room.

"Those are pretty," I said. "I didn't realize you were getting them already." Satella loved her bugs, and she often talked about the new ones she wanted. She never purchased pinned bugs that had been killed for their looks. She only wanted ones that had lived their proper life cycle.

"I know," she gushed. "It wasn't supposed to get here until fall, but it came early. Where do you think I should put it?" Her wine-colored eyes glimmered as she looked at the newest part of her collection.

The healer's walls were filled with pinned bugs. There wasn't much space for her to put the newest part of her collection.

"What about there?" I pointed to one of the few open spaces.

Satella set the frame down to look at where I pointed, but she caught a glimpse at me.

"Holy fuck. What happened to you?" She rushed over to me, forcing me to sit down in her patient's chair. "And why didn't you tell me to shut up about my bugs?"

"It's not as bad as it looks," I said. I didn't know if that was true, but I didn't want to worry anyone. My head throbbed, but my heart hurt worse.

Satella clicked her tongue. "Are you going to tell me what happened, or are you going to act like you know better than a healer?"

I narrowed my eyes, not appreciating the sass. "It was an accident."

"That's not a proper answer. Tell me now." She didn't hide the irritation in her voice—something she rarely showed to someone who wasn't her friend. She grabbed a glass bottle filled with a clear liquid. She poured a little onto a cloth before wiping the wound. I hissed as it made my forehead sting.

"I went to see the bleeding heart lily with Ovid." I paused, ashamed to tell the rest of the story.

Satella pinched her lips together as she studied my face. She knew there was more going on, so she kept her tone firm. "What happened?"

I looked down at my hands. "He said he would never ask a whale like me out. He only cared about seeing the flower. I was just someone he could use. When I realized that, I got angry and shoved him. He shoved me back, and I lost my balance. I hit my head on one of the tables, but it was an accident. I don't think he meant to hurt me."

Satella wrung the cloth, pure rage flashing in her eyes. "That man put his hands on you?" I had never heard Satella sound lethal before, but her tone made me shift in my seat. I never wanted to be on the other end of that rage.

"It was an accident." My voice was small. I wanted to believe Ovid wouldn't stoop to the level of physical harm. He was terrible, but I wanted to believe he wasn't *that* terrible. It was hard to swallow the fact that I had wasted years of my life crushing on someone who didn't like me back. I didn't want to believe he was also a terrible person on top of that.

"I don't *fucking* care. That man hurt you, and he deserves to die for it," Satella said. She pulled out a needle to stitch up my wound, but the ferocity of her movements made me take a step back.

"He doesn't love me. That's not a crime." I hated the words, even as they came out of my mouth. I wanted to be angry with Ovid for the way he spoke to me and treated me, but my chest was hollow. His words had been a painful reminder that on land I wasn't considered beautiful. If I wanted to go home, I could find plenty of mermen who were willing to marry me, but it was because of who I was, not just because voluptuous mermaids were considered attractive in the Hallow Sea. Not that I'd ever go back there.

Satella waved the threaded needle around, making me fear she'd accidentally stab me with her wild movements. "Don't defend him. He hurt you, physically and emotionally. That's why I fucking hate men."

There was no judgment in Satella's face, only anger towards the merchant. She didn't blame me or think less of me just because I liked someone who turned out to be terrible. I sat in front of her again and took a deep breath. "I hate them, too," I said, and it felt good. "I especially hate Ovid." That felt even better. I didn't want to defend him again. He didn't deserve it.

"This is why women are so much better," Satella said. She motioned for me to lean forward and stitched together the cut on my forehead.

"Sometimes I wonder if it'd be easier to find someone to love me if I liked women like that," I said. Women were beautiful, and they were easier to talk to, but I had never liked them like that.

"It's not," Satella said. "Dating women is easier, but it's easier to find men." Satella wrinkled her nose at the thought. She hadn't dated anyone since I arrived at Ethlow, but she had talked about the relationships she had over the centuries she had been alive. She was older than me and had more experience, but she looked like she was my age. That was the advantage of being immortal.

Mermaids lived longer than many other races, but I was considered a baby, despite being alive for over two decades. I didn't have much dating experience, and I was forced to keep the one relationship I had a secret. My parents were picky about who I dated, just another part of my life they controlled.

"Where did you go?" Satella asked, bringing me out of my thoughts.

I blinked several times, realizing she had already finished the stitching. She had deft fingers. "I was just wondering if I'd ever find someone to love me."

"Don't let that bastard merchant bring you down. You are beautiful and kind. Someone will see that and appreciate you. In fact, there's already someone who already sees you like that." Satella's lips curled in that way they did when she was ready to tease me, and I knew exactly who she was referring to.

I narrowed my eyes. "Don't go there."

"I'm just saying, no one actually eats that much. He goes to the kitchen too often." That wasn't the first time Satella had implied something similar.

"Stop it." I didn't think about a certain guardsman that way. He annoyed me with how much extra work he put me through, and we never hung out outside the kitchen. Not to mention we had gotten into a pretty big fight recently. There was no way he liked me like that.

Except he had worried when he saw the cut on my forehead. He put me before himself and his feelings.

No. That didn't mean anything. It was natural for friends to worry. Satella had had a similar reaction. It was dangerous to start thinking like that, especially with the way it had ended with Ovid.

"I'm just saying, I think Reamann likes you," Satella said. She wasn't going to drop the conversation easily.

"He's always asking me to make seafood. If he liked me, he wouldn't ask me, of all people, to do that," I said, reminding myself of all the days he annoyed me.

"Maybe he is just craving the taste of a certain sea maiden, so he's trying to fulfill it in whatever way he can."

My eyes widened at the implication. I had never thought about touching Reamann like that, especially not him... tasting me. I turned away from the vampire, unable to control the heat crawling up my cheeks. "You're wrong."

Satella giggled, delighted by my reaction. "I'm just saying—"

A soft knock on the door interrupted our conversation. Satella jumped up to open it. "Oh, Reamann, I wasn't expecting you." The way she said his name made me spin around.

His eyes immediately went to the bandaged wound on my head. "I just wanted to check on Aukina to make sure she's okay. Oh, and I wanted to let her know I finished unloading everything."

Satella glanced back at me with a knowing smirk, one I wanted to smack off her face. She stepped aside. "She's all yours."

Chapter 5

I had never felt awkward around Reamann before. Even when I was mad, it was easy to yell at him, but I couldn't get Satella's words out of my mind. What would it feel like to touch Reamann? To taste him?

I crossed my arms under my chest to stop myself from reaching over and grabbing his large, strong hand. I wondered what it'd feel like if he ran his hands over my body. Would they be rough? Smooth?

I bit my tongue, trying to stop those thoughts. I had just been hung up on Ovid. I didn't want to jump at the next male who paid any attention to me.

"Thanks for your help earlier," I said, hoping to break the tension that might have been all in my head.

"Anytime. I mean it. If you need anything, I'll be there." Reamann was kind, but I wished he wasn't. It would've been easier to erase the seeds Satella planted in my brain if he was cold to me.

We were nearly back to the kitchen, but I wasn't ready to part yet. Before we made it to the mess hall, I grabbed Reamann's arm. It was harder than I had imagined. I quickly crossed my arms again. "Wait."

Reamann paused, looking back at me. His eyes flicked down to my chest. I glanced down, realizing that crossing my arms accidentally pushed up my breasts. His face turned red as he realized he had been caught looking at me inappropriately. I dropped my arms and looked away from him.

"I never said sorry," I said, hoping to move past whatever that was.

"There's nothing for you to apologize for," Reamann said.

"That's not true. You were trying to be a good friend and warn me that Ovid wasn't a good guy. I didn't want to listen, but I shouldn't have treated you that way. I'm sorry."

When Reamann was quiet, I peeked through my curtain of hair. He stared at me, as if he was trying to decide how to respond.

"Tell you what. I'll forgive you on one condition," he said. "Get tomorrow off from cooking duty and meet me near the barracks at sunup."

"Why?" I rarely took a day off from the kitchen. I wasn't expected to work every day, but I feared everything would fall apart if I wasn't there, especially now that Cibil had slowed down. She rarely came around to give instructions.

"Can't tell you. That's part of the condition. So what do you say? Can you spare one day for me?" Reamann's red eyes glowed the way they did when he took the first bite of food he found particularly delicious, and I couldn't say no to him.

"I don't know if Cibil will be okay with me taking the entire day off," I said hesitantly.

Reamann leaned in, his face only a few inches away from mine. A sweet scent of berries clouded my thoughts. "I think they'll be fine. The old gnome has run the kitchen since the day the king opened his doors to others."

"Okay," I said, knowing I was going to give in. I had always given in to his whims.

Reamann snapped his spine straight, smiling brightly. "Great. See you first thing in the morning. Oh, and wear pants."

I tugged at my waist band as I finished preparing breakfast. Cibil had said I was free to take the day off and that I deserved a break, but I felt guilty leaving the head chef, Wistari, and the others to do all the work on short notice. I woke up before dawn to prepare as much as possible, which wasn't unusual for me. I liked the quiet mornings before the rest of the estate was awake. It was easier to work without distractions.

I hated wearing pants. It felt silly, since pants were more convenient. However, I preferred my dresses and skirts that covered my rounded stomach. It felt like it hid the rolls on my body, but there was no hiding in pants. I had to borrow a pair from Nyri, since I didn't own any, and she was the closest to my size.

"I thought I might find you here."

I screamed, dropping a pan on the floor. The metal clanging against the floor drowned out the pounding of my heart. I hadn't heard the orange-haired demon approach.

Reamann rushed over, reaching to grab the pan at the same time as me. Our hands brushed against each other, and I froze, looking up. The demon's eyes crinkled with amusement.

"You scared me," I said breathlessly.

Reamann chuckled. "I noticed."

I glared, but it was difficult to stay mad at him. I picked up the pan and set it on the counter. "What are you doing here, anyway? I thought I was meeting you at the barracks at sunup. It's not even light out yet."

Reamann leaned against the counter and ran his hand through his hair. It was damp, as if he had just bathed. Instead of his normal armor, he wore a simple, white shirt that was cut into a V-shape at the neck, revealing the top of his muscular pecs.

"I got off my shift early, and I had a feeling you were going to squeeze in as much work as possible before meeting up, so I thought I'd steal you away early." He grabbed the back of his neck, making his muscles flex.

I swallowed hard, confused by the thrum in my core. I had never looked at Reamann like *that* before. I turned to the counter to focus on my prep work. "That's not going to happen. I agreed to sunup, so you can either help me finish this, or you can wait by the barracks until the sun rises."

Reamann moved next to me, the chill from his body brushing against my heated skin, making me painfully aware of his closeness. "Tell me what to do."

I had expected him to tell me he'd see me later, so his response threw me off. I grabbed a large wooden spoon and shoved it into his hand. "Mix this until all the ingredients are incorporated."

I watched him for a moment, and when I decided he was doing it correctly, I moved on to prepare the next batch of muffins. We worked together until the counters were filled with fresh muffins, finishing just before the sun was ready to crest the horizon. Our hard work lined the counter. It wasn't enough to get Cibil and the rest of the kitchen staff through the day, but it'd make breakfast easier for them.

"Do you do this every day?" Reamann wiped his forehead, but it only left flour in the wake of his hand.

I walked over to him and lifted onto my toes to wipe the flour off his face. "Most days, yes. I like preparing easy stuff for people to eat, just in case they are in a hurry. I don't always wake up this early, though."

"You're incredible," he breathed, reminding me of how close we were.

I pulled my hand back quickly and stepped away. "It's a lot of work to keep the estate fed, but I like it. Seeing people enjoy my food brings me joy, but it's nothing compared to what you do. You keep the estate safe."

"Most days we sit around on our asses, waiting for something to happen." Reamann laughed. "It's rare that something is stupid enough to attack the demon king's estate. It's even rarer for someone to attack it. The demon king's power can be felt outside the gates."

"You're risking your life. The most I'm risking is a burn." I looked at my hands. Over the years, I had collected small scars from long days in the kitchen. My hands were no longer the delicate fingers my family had tried hard to maintain.

"Don't underestimate yourself," Reamann said. "Without you, the estate would starve." He grabbed my hand, and a jolt ran up my arm. "Now that the sun is up, we need to get going."

My heart raced as the demon pulled me out of the kitchen. "You haven't said where we're going."

"You'll see."

The sun peeked over the horizon, indicating it was safe to go outside. It was warm, despite the early morning, which meant the afternoon heat would be intense. I shouldn't have agreed to go out during the summer, but there was no going back now.

Reamann didn't stop until we reached the backside of the barracks where the stables were kept. Several horses looked at us as we approached. A sinking feeling twisted in my gut as Reamann stopped in front of two horses that had already been saddled. He let go of my hand to check on the horses, and I took the opportunity to take a step back.

The white horse stared at me, as if it could see right into my soul. I took another small step back, wondering how long it'd take Reamann to notice if I bolted for the estate.

"This here is Tatzy," he said, gesturing to the white spotted horse, "and this is Hakka." He petted the brown horse on the neck.

"We're not going anywhere with them, right?" My heart drummed against my ribs so loudly I was sure Reamann heard the erratic pattern.

"Oh, we definitely are." He patted Hakka's neck, and the horse bobbed its nose in approval.

I took a step back. "No, thanks. I don't do horses."

Reamann furrowed his eyebrows. "Why not? They're really nice."

I was sure he thought that was true, but it didn't change anything for me. "I have never ridden a horse, and I don't plan to start today." In the sea, we didn't rely on other creatures to get around. Our tails were faster than any sea creature worth taming.

Reamann stepped away from the creatures. "Are you scared of horses?"

Scared was an understatement. "I don't ride giant, four-legged creatures that could kill me."

"Do you ride creatures with less legs?" Reamann asked, lifting a single eyebrow.

"No." I had heard of people using wyverns as mounts, but that seemed worse than a horse. It was one aspect about land dwellers that I struggled to understand.

"I swear I won't let any harm come to you." Reamann held out his hand. "Do you trust me?"

I wanted to say no. If I didn't trust him, then I could turn around and never have to deal with a horse. However, saying no would be a lie. My chest deflated, knowing I was once again weak to the charms of the demon in front of me. I took his hand, trying not to show just how terrified I was.

Reamann smiled, squeezing my hand delicately. "I promise you won't regret this."

Part of me already did.

Chapter 6

I could hardly breathe as I clung to the saddle in front of me. My thighs squeezed the horse, unable to relax, even as my muscles burned. I didn't dare loosen my grip. Reamann had magic powers. It was the only explanation as to how he had managed to get me on such a large creature.

"You can relax a little," Reamann said in my ear. His voice in my ear made my body more tense.

He sat behind the saddle, since there wasn't room for both of us in the leather seat. I refused to ride alone, so it was the only way he had convinced me to get on the beast in the first place.

"That's not happening," I muttered. If the beast decided it was done with us on its back, it could easily fling us off, either hurting or killing us in the process. I had seen the horse-related injuries Satella dealt with, and I didn't want to know what that was like first hand.

"If you don't unclench your muscles, you're going to be insanely sore tomorrow." I knew he was right. I already felt the soreness building up in my legs, but the fear coursing through my system made it impossible to calm down.

"Yep." Knowing I needed to relax and actually relaxing were two completely different beasts.

"Here. Take the reins." Reamann shoved the leather straps guiding the horses into my hands."

"Wh-what are you doing?" I stammered. I wanted to jump off the horse and get as far away from it as possible. If I wasn't worried that the beast would react poorly, I wouldn't have thought twice.

"Helping you relax." His breath brushed against my ear, having the opposite effect. My heart stuttered, and my mind raced as my body felt things it shouldn't. Reamann was a friend. Nothing more. I barely considered him a friend a week ago. Before Ovid rejected me, I wouldn't have thought anything about his actions, but between the merchant's cruel words and Satella's teasing, all I could think about was Reamann touching me in ways friends didn't touch each other.

Reamann placed his hands on my hips, and I was grateful he couldn't see the look on my face.

"Take a deep breath," he ordered, his lips only an inch away from my ear.

The breath I took was shaky and shallow.

Reamann chuckled, his laugh vibrating in my chest. "Either you don't know what a deep breath is, or you're just really bad at breathing."

I would've glared at him if he could have seen my face. Instead, I forced air into my lungs as deeply as possible and let the breath out slowly to prove him wrong.

"That's a good girl." His hands moved down from my hips to my thighs. "Now take another deep breath and focus on loosening your muscles. I don't want you to be completely useless later."

I licked my lips and swallowed hard. I liked his praise more than I ever wanted to admit. "For what?"

"You'll see."

I closed my eyes and took another deep breath. I had to get my mind out of the hole it had fallen into. There was no way Reamann meant *that*. Another deep breath, and I relaxed. A little.

"Good," he said. "Now I want you to focus on the sound of the horse's hooves on the grass. Listen to the wind in the trees. Horses are living creatures, just like you and me. They don't mean any harm."

The breeze tickled my face, and Reamann's fingers warmed my thighs. The rhythm of the horse's hooves felt like a steady drum, and suddenly, it wasn't as scary. My body relaxed, leaning into Reamann's torso. My heart rate slowed for the first time since seeing the horses, and for a moment, I saw how others could find horseback riding enjoyable.

The horse neighed, making that feeling wash away in an instant. I bolted up right, but Reamann wrapped his arms around my torso, securing me against him.

"It's okay," he said. "We're here."

A light from a lake reflected into my eyes. "I didn't know there was a lake here." After arriving at Ethlow, I hadn't explored outside the estate. It was hard to go anywhere when I spent every day in the kitchen.

"I thought that might be the case." Reamann took the reins from me and slowed the horse to a stop. He swung off the back and turned with his hands up, as if to help me down.

"What are you doing?" I asked slowly. I had insisted on getting on the horse on my own, and I planned on getting down the same way.

"There are no steps for you to use. Swing your leg over, and I'll help you down." He didn't move as he waited for me to follow his instructions.

I didn't move, either. "I can get down on my own."

"It's pretty high up, and I don't want you to get hurt." He moved a little closer, but it didn't make me feel better.

I tightened my grip on the saddle. I was scared to get off on my own, but having Reamann help felt worse. "I... I can figure it out."

"This is your first time on a horse, and you're scared. It'll be better if I help you." The determination in his eyes told me he wasn't going to back down.

I didn't want to be honest with him, but I didn't feel like I had a choice. "I'm too heavy for you to carry." I swallowed hard, embarrassed by the truth. The extra weight had never been an issue in the sea. I moved freely without gravity pulling me down in the water, but on land, it was different. I was too heavy for others to carry, something I had learned during the time I spent on the Nescen Islands. Ever since, I did everything on my own to avoid that same kind of embarrassment.

Reamann's face softened, but he didn't lower his hands. "Do you think I'm that weak?"

"I know I'm that heavy." A different kind of panic gripped my throat. I wished I had refused to come on this adventure with Reamann. Then I wouldn't have had to ride a horse or face the reality of my excess weight.

"Do you trust me?" he asked.

I pulled my lips between my teeth. I hated it when he asked me that question, because there was only one honest response. "Yes."

He placed a hand on my thigh. "Then let me help you down."

I hesitated, not wanting Reamann to feel just how heavy I was. It was one thing for him to see my body. It was another for him to feel it.

"Aukina." His voice was soft, pulling my attention to him. "I see you, okay?"

His red eyes burned into mine, leaving an impression that was lasting. I gave him a nod, finally giving in. The alternative was to live on the horse, which was worse. "Okay," I whispered.

I swung my leg over the saddle, but looking down from that angle made it nearly impossible to move.

"I'm here," Reamann said. If I fell, I'd fall directly on him, which was both comforting and horrifying.

I had no choice if I wanted to get off the horse. I tried to lower myself slowly, but my arms were too weak to move the way I wanted to. I squeezed my eyes shut, preparing to fall, but Reamann's strong arms caught me. My hands automatically went to his shoulders, desperate to hold onto something. He lowered me to the ground at a perfectly controlled speed. I opened my eyes once my feet were securely on the ground.

He kept his hands on my side. "See. You're not too heavy at all." His smile made my heart stutter.

I didn't know what was wrong with me. Reamann was only a friend. He could never love someone like me, especially when he didn't know who I really was, but as he smiled at me, it was easy to imagine a different world. One where he was so much more than just a friend.

Reamann was the first to pull away. He grabbed the reins of the horse and led Hakka to a tree where he tied her up. I couldn't move as he grabbed supplies from the saddlebags, even though I felt like I should help him. Instead, I looked at his defined muscles flexing as he grabbed several bags. He was stronger than he looked. He had to be. He was one of the guardsmen responsible for protecting Ethlow. He had to fight monsters and intruders who tried to disturb the peace of the demon king's estate.

"You coming?" Reamann called out, motioning towards the lake with his head, since his hands were full.

My feet remembered how to move, and I scurried to join him. "Do you need help carrying anything?"

"I got it." Despite several bags in his hands, he didn't break a sweat as we walked to the lake.

When we were close to the shore, he set the bag down, pulling out a large, quilted blanket. He laid it on the ground, and I jumped in to help straighten the corners. Then he unpacked several food items and laid them out in an unorganized mess. There were wraps, fruit, cheese, and even a bottle of a dark purple liquid.

"When did you prepare all this?" I asked. Usually requests for food went through me, but I hadn't heard anything about this.

"Nyri gave me the fruit from her garden, and Malse made the wraps, and Wistari helped with everything else. It was a bit of a group effort." The orange-haired demon scratched the back of his neck nervously.

If I hadn't known better, I would've guessed that Reamann had been planning this outing for longer than a day, but that didn't make sense.

"It looks incredible." I sat on the blanket, trying to ignore the swelling in my chest. I couldn't remember the last time someone had prepared food for me when they weren't paid to do so.

"It does?" Reamann sat next to me, watching me with giant puppy dog eyes.

"It does," I said. I grabbed two wraps, handing one to Reamann and keeping one for myself. I was starving after the long journey. "I can't believe you did all of this." I didn't know what else to say.

"I don't know what that jerk merchant said to you, but I saw how much it hurt you. I thought getting you away for a day would be good for you, and since you're a mermaid, I figured a lake would be the perfect spot."

"So you *do* realize I'm a mermaid." I shook my head. It was impossible to hide my mermaid nature, even when I had legs. The gills on my neck were always present, and my sharp teeth gave away my true nature. Yet, the guard often seemed oblivious to the fact.

Reamann's face went blank. "What do you mean? Of course, I know that."

I looked down at the wrap. "Then why are you always asking me to make you seafood?" When he first started making trips to the kitchen, I was happy to fulfill his requests. It wasn't long before it had become an annoyance, but somewhere along the line, it had been comforting—except when he asked me to chop up fish for him.

My question only seemed to confuse him more. "What's wrong with that?"

"I'm a mermaid from the sea, and you want me to make *sea*food. I grew up with fish friends." I watched as his face shifted from confusion to one of horror, and I felt a laugh bubbling up.

"I swear I never meant to insult you." I had never seen him that pale before, and I couldn't stop the chuckle from spilling over, which shifted his face back to confusion. "Why are you laughing?"

"Because you look like you just realized you've committed a crime. You're cute when you look guilty." I slammed my mouth shut, realizing what had just escaped. Friends didn't call each other cute—not like that. And we were just friends.

"Because I have committed a crime. If I knew it bothered you, I never would've asked for that."

"It's fine," I said. "For you, it's worth it." I let my statement sink in, realizing it was true. Even as he annoyed me over the years, Reamann was my favorite person to feed. Watching the euphoria on his face when he ate my food warmed my heart, even when he ate seafood.

Several moments passed with neither of us saying anything, but it was a comfortable silence. I was always comfortable with Reamann, something I had taken for granted.

"We should eat before it gets late," I said.

"Right." Reamann blinked a few times, as if he was pulling himself out of a stupor.

At the same time, we took a bite of our food. Reamann's face twisted, before the horror hit my tongue. I immediately spit out the wrap, but there was a grainy texture stuck to my tongue that tasted like dirt. I pulled the wrap open, and between the layers of meat and cheese, there was sand. I looked up at Reamann ready for an explanation, but he looked as confused as me. Then he clenched his jaw.

"I should've known better than to ask that goblin for help," he muttered.

I wiped my tongue on the back of my hand, trying to get as much of the dirt out of my mouth as possible. "Okay, I'm going to need an explanation, because I don't know anyone who thinks dirt is tasty."

"Sorry," Reamann said, his cheeks turning pink. "I sort of have a prank war with Malse. I should've known better than to ask for their help, but I thought if they knew it was for you, they'd behave."

Malse was the head seamstress at Ethlow. I didn't know much about her, but she always looked serious when I saw her. For a moment, I wasn't sure if Reamann was serious, but then I thought back to the time when he showed up in a pink shirt. He had said it was a prank, but I brushed it off. "Wait, you actually got into a prank war with the head seamstress?"

"It started out as a simple jest, but I wasn't expecting the goblin to return fire." Reamann hung his head in shame. "I ruined this, didn't I?"

"No, you didn't ruin anything." I reached over and touched Reamann's hand, wanting to reassure him, but when a spark ran through my fingers, I felt a shift in the air. I had known Reamann for years, but I was starting to realize I never really knew him.

Chapter 7

R eamann stretched his arms high above his head and leaned
back until he was lying on the blanket. He closed his eyes,
taking in the sun. I watched his chest move up and down slowly.
He looked at peace, as if he didn't have a worry in the world. I
wondered what it'd feel like to be that kind of free. No worries
about the past coming back to haunt me. No worries about my
weight and looks. No worries about what was happening back in
the kitchen and if everyone was fed.

"How did someone like you end up at Ethlow?" I asked, my
voice breaking the silence.

Reamann cracked his eyes open, looking at me out of the corner
of his eyes. "Someone like me?"

"Yeah, someone so sweet and caring." Those at Ethlow were
rejected from the world in one way or another. Or they were like
me, running away from a life they didn't want. No matter who
showed up at the demon king's estate, we all had a haunted past or
a sour personality. Reamann didn't look like he belonged, but we
all had our stories.

He rolled onto his side and propped his head with his arm. "I'm
a demon, remember? We're not exactly welcome in most societies.

There are not many places for a demon to live comfortably outside Ethlow."

"You don't look like a demon, though. I don't think I've ever seen you with horns or wings or a tail." I reached over and ruffled his hair without thinking to prove my point.

Reamann closed his eyes as my fingers tangled in his hair. It made me want to never stop touching him. "That's because you've only seen me during the day."

"What does that have to do with anything?" Other demons at the estate had their extra features showing throughout the day. They didn't have control over their horns, but more powerful demons were an exception, like the demon king. The more power they had, the easier it was for them to change in and out of demon form at will, even varying the level of demon-ness. I had thought Reamann was a lesser demon, since his power didn't ripple off him the way it flowed from Viridian or the demon king, but maybe I was wrong.

Reamann rolled on his back, pulling away from my hand. "I'm only half-demon. My mother is a demon, but my father was a human. Because of that, I look like a human during the day, but after dark, my body shifts into its demon form. I can't control it, which made it tricky to live with my father. He allowed me out of the house during the day, but I had to be home before dark, so the villagers didn't find out the truth. I was always good about it, until I wasn't. I was only a few minutes late, but that was all it took."

He closed his eyes, haunted memories attacking the muscles on his face. He took a deep breath, and then he sat up suddenly. When he looked at me, his eyes were breathtaking.

"I left the next day," Reamann said.

I wanted to ask about his mother and what happened to her, but I was afraid to ask. He had his reasons for not bringing her up on his own, and it wasn't my place to pry.

I didn't know what to say, so I leaned over and grabbed his hand. Reamann squeezed my hand, and we sat there for a moment, neither of us wanting to part. Then Reamann asked, "So what about you? How does a mermaid end up at a place like Ethlow?"

I took my hand away, shame filling my bones. I ran away for selfish reasons, but I didn't have the right to hide my secrets, not when Reamann had just spilled his.

"I had no good reason to run away," I admitted. "I had a good life in a well-known family. My future was set, but that was the problem. My parents had every part of my life planned out, including who I was going to marry and how many children I was going to have. One day, I couldn't take it anymore, so I swam away. I left the sea for land, knowing they wouldn't look for me here, and if they did, it'd be harder for them to find me. I struggled without the sea, but a fairy told me that I could live in Ethlow as long as I did my share of work. I haven't looked back since."

Without my tail, my family couldn't sense my presence, like they could if I stayed in the sea. It was the only way to guarantee they wouldn't drag me back against my will.

I played with the ends of my hair, not wanting to see the judgment in Reamann's face. "Seems pretty pathetic compared to you, huh?"

"No," he said simply. "You felt suffocated and didn't have any freedom. I can't imagine what that was like."

The water called out to me, and I found myself gazing at the lake, longing to be submerged in water. "My family claimed they needed me, but my sister is the eldest, so she'll take over the bloodline when my parents retire. I'm sure they are perfectly fine without me. " I was a coward, something my family couldn't afford. Sometimes I thought about what it'd be like to go home, but I couldn't stand the thought of being under my mother's shark-like ruling.

"Do you ever think about going back home?" Reamann asked. His voice was gentle, lacking the judgment I had come to expect.

I hadn't told Satella or Nyri the truth about who I was or why I ran away, afraid they'd look at me differently, but it was different with Reamann. He was easy to talk to. "Sometimes," I admitted. "I miss my papa, even though he never understood my fascination with the land. My sister was insufferable at times, but she would sit with me under the full moon just to keep me company. I think I miss the sea the most. I miss the freedom of my tail."

I wiggled my toes, but they were hidden beneath the boots strapped to my feet.

"When's the last time you shifted to your mermaid form?" Reamann asked.

"Over five years ago, after I ran away from home and before I made it to Ethlow. I accidentally got caught in a rainstorm, and I was forced to change. I have avoided it since." I didn't know if it was my tail or the sea that allowed my family to sense my presence, so I went to extreme lengths to avoid both. I gave myself sponge baths to prevent the change. My body had a threshold for how wet it could get before I exchanged legs for a tail.

"Maybe it's time you stopped avoiding it." Reamann jumped to his feet and held out his hand.

My heart picked up pace as I looked back and forth between Reamann and the water. My body craved the sensation of being fully submerged, but the fear in the pit of my stomach made me freeze.

Years of hiding from my past.

Years of hiding from myself.

Years of running and pretending and denying a part of myself.

I took Reamann's hand, and he pulled me to my feet. He didn't let go as he smiled, shining brighter than the sun. My heart raced, but for a different reason. The orange-haired demon had been in my life for years, but it was as if a fire had been lit, changing everything.

Reamann led me to the water, never letting go of my hand. He stopped on the shore, just before the sand turned into water. "Only if you want to," he said as a gentle reminder.

My breath was shaky. Shifting gave my family the chance to find me, but it had nearly been six years since I'd left. I prayed to Artagatis that even if they could sense me, they wouldn't bother to find me. "I want to." I wanted to more than he could understand.

I pulled off my shirt, letting it drop to the ground. I worked on untying my pants next, my heart picking up pace as I stood in just my brassiere and underwear. Mermaids weren't shy with their bodies. The sea wasn't a place to hide beneath clothes. I used to lounge on the sand with nothing covering me but my hair, but the years on the land had infected my carefree attitude.

I glanced at Reamann, chewing on my lip as I debated about asking him to turn away. I was afraid of him seeing me completely nude, but there was no going back. I took off my brassiere before pulling my long, black hair to cover my chest. I removed my bottoms, too afraid to see the expression on the demon's face. There were no clothes to cover the rolls on my body, and I didn't know if I'd see disgust or something else entirely. I wasn't ready to know.

The water was cold against my toes as I took a step forward, but it felt wonderful. The sea was colder than this lake, even during the long summer days, which was why I preferred winters on land. The summer air made my blood boil, since mermaids thrived in the cold, but with each step I took, the cool water soothed my nerves.

The moment the water hit half my body, a spark ran through my spine. My legs merged together, shifting into a tail. My body collapsed, and my head went under the water. The gills on my neck flared, my body instantly remembering how to breathe underwater. A surge of energy pulsed through my veins, and for a moment, all of my worries disappeared.

I moved through the water, twisting and turning without the restraints of gravity. I felt as if I was flying, and it'd be easy to disappear in the water, never returning to my human form.

A muffled shout from the surface pulled my attention. Splashes in the water grew louder, and I felt panic pulse through the lake, as if it was part of my nervous system. I poked my head out of the water, and Reamann was in the lake, fully clothed. He stopped when he saw me, but his chest heaved up and down, his eyes wide.

"You're okay," he breathed, talking to himself more than me. "You were under for so long, I thought..." His voice trailed off. I hadn't realized I had been under long enough to worry him.

I gestured to my neck. "Mermaids can breathe underwater."

Reamann scratched the back of his neck. His cheeks tinged pink. "Right. I forgot for a moment."

I swam up to Reamann with complete control over my body. I stopped mere inches away from him. I had been trapped in my land body for so long, I had forgotten the freedom that came with a tail. "You got your clothes wet."

Reamann looked taller from this angle, since only my head came out of the water, and he stood waist deep.

"Oops." His chuckle was light and careless. He grabbed his shirt and pulled it off his head. He tossed it to the shore, leaving his torso completely bare. My fingers itched to feel the smooth ridges of his muscles.

I swam backwards, needing space to clear my head. Despite the cool water, it felt like there was a fire burning in my veins.

Reamann waded deeper in the water, slowly closing the gap between us. He stopped just before his collarbones were submerged. He didn't take his eyes off me once. "How does it feel to be free again?"

I smiled without a thought. Leaning back, I let the water support my body. My hair floated around me, and I no longer cared if it was covering me or not. I was free for the first time in too long.

"Your tail is the second most beautiful thing I've seen," Reamann said.

I wasn't a stranger to compliments on my tail. The cerulean scales reflected the light, shifting between blues and greens. The color was rare among mermaids. It was considered an ideal color for a mate, since it was the perfect color to blend in with the deep sea if there was ever any danger.

"What's the most beautiful thing you've seen?" I asked, unable to contain my curiosity.

"You." He said it with full confidence.

I cracked my eyes open, and Reamann was looking at my face. Not my tail. Not my exposed breasts. My face.

"What?" I felt like an idiot the moment the word came out of my mouth.

"The first day I saw you in the kitchen, you stunned me into silence with your beauty. Your eyes were kind, and your smile was welcoming and friendly, and I knew I had to get to know you, but I didn't know what to say. So I made up reasons to see you. That's why I come to the kitchen as often as I do. I just wanted to see you."

I couldn't find my voice. All this time, Reamann wasn't bothering me because he had an insatiable appetite. He wanted to see *me*. I didn't know what to say. How could I have been so blind?

Reamann inched closer, his fingers hovering in the water near my body. I couldn't catch my breath as I thought about the way his fingers would feel on my skin.

"Do you want to touch my tail?" It was a strange question after Reamann's confession. It wasn't a declaration of love. It wasn't exactly a declaration of like, either, but it gave me the courage to be bold.

When he hesitated, I grabbed his hand and brought it to my scales. "It's okay," I said.

He slid his fingers over the scales, taking his time until he reached the area that would've been the side of my thigh. My scales tingled beneath his touch. It was considered an intimate gesture to touch a merfolk's tail, but it wasn't common knowledge outside the sea.

"It's softer than I expected." Reamann's fingers continued moving up, running along the side of my body. When his fingers crossed over from tail to hip, my breath hitched. He continued moving up my side, and I didn't stop him. I never wanted him to stop.

He watched my face the entire time, looking for any indication that he had crossed a line, but he wouldn't find one. He moved even higher, his fingers gently tracing the side of my breast. I ached for him to linger there, to massage my chest with his calloused fingers. It had been too long since someone had touched me like that, and his fingers ignited a fire in my core. He continued up my neck until his fingers cupped my cheek. He leaned forward, and my eyes fluttered shut.

For a brief moment, the world was thick with anticipation. I didn't breathe as I waited, hoping he was doing what I assumed. His lips pressed against mine, soft and gentle, leaving me aching for more. Something I hadn't felt in a long time filled my chest. Joy and hope, and I was hooked.

Chapter 8

I couldn't stop smiling. I felt like a guppy with her first crush. The kiss hadn't lasted long, and nothing else had happened, but that didn't matter. Every time I looked at Reamann, my smile grew brighter, making my cheeks ache.

I sat on the shore, squeezing out the excess water from my hair. Reamann tried to wring out his pants, but there was only so much he could do to dry them before the journey back to Ethlow. I pulled my shirt over my head and waited for the rest of my body to dry enough for my tail to shift back into legs.

"How long does the transformation take?" Reamann asked after he pulled his pants back on.

I flicked the fins on the end of my tail, still coming down from the high of being in the water. "Depends. Once I'm dry enough, it happens pretty quickly." I shielded my eyes from the sun as I looked out onto the water, ignoring the urge to get back in. "With how warm it is, it shouldn't take long."

He plopped down next to me and leaned back. Little droplets ran down his torso. The sun glistened against the water, drying them quickly. I resisted the urge to reach out and run my fingers over the smooth ridges.

"We still have some time before we have to make our way back, since the sun has been setting later," Reamann said. The summer solstice was only a few weeks away, and the days had been growing longer. Many of the residents loved the summer, because they could spend more time outside without breaking the rules.

I rarely spent time outside during the summer. My body functioned better in the cold, so summers were rough. As my body dried and the heat became more intense, the urge to go back into the water only grew. I didn't know when I'd be able to get away from the kitchen again to come back to the lake, but I wasn't afraid anymore. I didn't want to run from my mermaid side.

"Thank you for today," I said. "It was exactly what I needed. I can't remember the last time I spent the day out of the kitchen."

"You looked like you needed it. After what that merchant did..." He dug his fingers into the sand. "I don't think I've ever seen you that upset, and I wanted to do something to make you smile."

I turned towards the demon, and he was already looking at me. My heart thumped, scared and excited all at once. I didn't know what the kiss had meant, but I was eager to find out. "The only thing that would've made this perfect is if we didn't have to ride that horse back to the estate."

Reamann laughed, shaking his head. "I never would've expected a mermaid to be afraid of horses. Hakka won't hurt you. I swear."

"We all have fears. I'm sure there's something that you're afraid of."

"Nope. There's no reason to be afraid. The world is a mix of good and bad, and what will happen will happen. I don't like to waste my time being afraid of something I can't change."

I crossed my arms and huffed, feeling a little defensive. "Well, not everyone can be fearless like you. Most regular people have fears, whether it's spiders, heights, or horses."

"I know," Reamann said. "And there's nothing wrong with that."

I narrowed my eyes. "There has to be something you're afraid of. Death?"

Reamann shrugged. "Everyone dies, even the immortal. When—if my time comes, it's a natural part of life."

"There has to be something."

"You can search all you want, but you won't find anything." He leaned in, leaving only a few inches between our faces. "But that's okay. It just means I can protect you from everything that scares you."

The teasing mood shifted into something softer, and I found myself leaning in, wanting another taste of him. Reamann cupped my cheek, closing the rest of the distance between us. His thumb brushed my face as our lips melded together, lasting longer than last time. My entire body melted into his touch, and I found myself craving more. I wanted him to touch me everywhere.

Suddenly, my skin tightened, and my scales disappeared. In a few seconds, my tail disappeared, leaving two legs in its place. I jolted from the sudden sensation, and Reamann pulled back. At first, he panicked, but his face relaxed once he realized what had happened. His eyes scanned my bare legs, moving higher and higher. I squeezed my thighs together, heat gathering between them as I thought about what it'd be like to spread my legs for the demon.

"We should head back," Reamann whispered, as if he was fighting for control over himself.

"Right," I whispered back, struggling to pull my desires back to the depths where they had lain dormant for too long.

During the entire ride back to Ethlow, Reamann had his hands wrapped around my waist. My fear of horses lingered, but I felt safe with him holding me. It was as if, even if something bad happened, I knew he'd be there. When we made it back to the estate, the sun was low in the sky, preparing for the night. This time I didn't fight Reamann when he lifted me off the horse, setting me gently on the ground. He kept his hands on my hips, smiling down at me. It didn't feel real. After the cruel things Ovid said to me, having Reamann hold me and kiss me as if I was special to him felt like a dream.

"I should get back to the kitchen," I said, but I didn't move my hands from his shoulders. I wasn't ready to dive back into reality.

"I should go, too." Reamann didn't move, either. He slid his hands higher on my waist, pulling me closer. "But I don't want to yet."

"Me neither," I admitted. I leaned in and batted my eyelids, wanting him to kiss me again, but I didn't want to say it out loud.

Reamann dipped his head closer to me, as if reading my mind, but before his lips reached mine, shouting interrupted us. Wistari yelled my name over and over as she bolted towards us. Her panic flipped a switch in me, and I rushed towards her as fast as I could.

"What's going on?" I asked, grabbing the young elf's arms.

"Come quick. Everything is being destroyed." She dragged me with her, heading straight to the kitchen.

As we entered the back door of the mess hall, I heard shouting in a language I didn't understand and the clattering of metal against stone. I rushed to the kitchen, unable to process what was happening. I flung the staff door open, and a knife thunked into the wall next to me. I should've taken a step back, but my kitchen was being destroyed.

Viridian held another knife in his hands, and his teal eyes glowed with rage. I had never seen the master of the house show any kind of emotion other than mild irritation. He was skilled at staying composed, but dark shadows fluttered out of his aura. The air was sticky with his killing intent. I should've run from the enraged demon. He was too dangerous to face, since I didn't have magic or any fighting skills. I was a fish out of water when it came to protecting myself.

"What's going on?" I demanded with as much moxie as I could manage.

A squeak pulled my attention as a rat scurried over the kitchen counter. Viridian growled and threw the knife, missing the small creature and hitting a bag of flour instead. Flour poured into the air in a puff. I yelped, jumping backwards. The demon already had another knife, as if he had an endless stream of weapons at his disposal. The damage done to my kitchen was proof of that. But what I didn't understand was why the master of the house attacked the rat with simple weapons. He was a powerful demon that could've eviscerated the rodent with a snap of his fingers.

"What in the devil?" Reamann muttered as he stopped behind me.

I barely paid attention to him, scanning the kitchen for an idea. If the rat continued to go free, my kitchen would be demolished. There was no reason for the damage, but Viridian wasn't acting with reason.

The rat was moving in a line on the counter, but it was running out of its runway. Another knife was thrown, missing its target. I had to do something quickly to stop the powerful demon from destroying everything. Then I saw a mixing bowl, and I knew what I had to do.

"We should get out of here," Reamann said.

I rushed into the kitchen, figuring I had seconds before the next attack. I swiped the bowl and moved as fast as I could. The rat jumped off the counter, and another knife flew through the air, missing me by a fraction of an inch. Reamann and Wistari shouted from the other side of the room. I shut out the chaos and slammed the bowl down as my knees hit the ground. My chest heaved, fear and adrenaline mixing together.

Viridian hovered over me, the shadows around him growing and sucking the oxygen out of the air. He held a knife next to his head, ready to strike. "Move, so I can kill the vermin."

I froze, unable to respond. The master of the house looked ready to slit my throat. Reamann rushed forward, stopping between Viridian and me.

"We'll take care of the rat," Reamann said, blocking me with his body.

Viridian's lips curled. Silence pulsed with his rage, as if he was debating about killing Reamann and me to get to the rat. "Make sure that thing is dead. If I ever see it inside this estate again, you will be the ones I punish." With a flick of his wrist, the knife disappeared into the shadows. The master of the house walked away, straightening his shirt and composing himself. When he reached the door, he turned back, making direct eye contact with me. "If this place falls apart when you're gone for a few hours, we have a problem. We will discuss it later. And Reamann, your shift starts soon. Don't be late." Then the demon disappeared in the shadows.

My shoulders slumped. My kitchen was destroyed, and it felt like my fault. The magic from today disappeared in a flash. The frown carved into Reamann's face told me that he felt the same way.

Reamann crouched in front of me. "Want me to take care of that for you?" He gestured to the rat under the bowl.

The rodent looked up at me through the clear glass. One eye was red and the other was yellow, and it looked sad—if that was even possible for a rat. "I don't want to kill it." It made no sense. If the rat found its way back to the estate, Viridian would blame me, and I didn't want to find out what the consequences were. But it was an innocent creature roaming into the kitchen just to get food. It didn't deserve death.

Reamann put his hand on mine. "Then we won't kill it."

"But if it finds its way back to the estate—"

"We will make sure it's far enough away." He squeezed my hand and smiled, making my heart soften.

"Doesn't your shift start soon?" I didn't know why I was fighting him. I was grateful for his help, but I was used to doing everything on my own.

He glanced out the window, taking a moment to gauge the time. "It's about an hour before sundown. We have time."

Reamann grabbed a cutting board and carefully pushed it under the bowl, trapping the rat. We stepped over broken chairs and shattered dishes to get out of the estate. Neither of us spoke as we left the estate grounds, walking for as long as time allowed us. The air felt heavy, Viridian's words lingering in my ears. I took one day off, and the kitchen turned into a disaster. I had to make the kitchen my priority, but the more time I spent with the demon next to me, the less I wanted to spend in the kitchen.

Reamann was the first one to stop walking. "I think this is far enough."

I glanced back, unable to see the estate through the forest. "Let's hope so."

He set the cutting board on the ground and then slowly lifted the bowl. The rat scurried out, running away from the estate. It had learned its lesson. As I watched him run off to freedom, a weight fell off my shoulders.

Caw!

A crow flew through the trees, calling out to the world. It swooped down, clutching the rat in its claws before flying away with the rodent. My mouth fell open as the bird flew away. The attempt to save the rat was pointless.

"At least we don't have to worry about it getting back into the kitchen," Reamann said. He was trying to cheer me up, but it didn't work. It felt as if the crow was a sign, as if everything was on the verge of falling apart.

"We should get back," I said. Reamann's face tightened, a darkness looming between us, but I didn't want the day to end that way. I slipped my fingers between his and squeezed his hand. He squeezed back, and my heart stuttered.

I didn't understand my feelings for Reamann. They were new, but they made me want to spend every moment with him. It was more intense than the feelings for Ovid ever were. With the merchant, it was a fantasy, something to think about in spare moments. With Reamann, it was as if a tree collapsed on top of me, but I was ready for it to crush me.

Chapter 9

My body ached in ways I never thought possible. My thighs burned from the horse ride, and my core was sore from using my tail for the first time in years. The worst part was bending over to grab supplies or clean the kitchen. Wistari helped me as much as she could, but even with the two of us, it took all morning to get the kitchen back to a usable condition. The damage to the wall wasn't something I could fix, which meant I had to submit a request to the building repair crew.

"Where's the hot breakfast today?" The sharp voice made my body tense. Of all days, today was the worst one for Tiafel to be in a mood. The fae was the closest thing to an enemy that I had. Her red hair hung in perfect strands around her face, and her make-up was perfect—as it was every day. She wore a corset that accentuated her thin waist and curvy hips. If she had a nicer personality, I would've been jealous of her looks.

I turned to the fae and plastered on my best fake smile. Tiafel had tested my patience enough that I had become skilled at pretending to be nice to her. I leaned on the counter that separated the kitchen from the rest of the mess hall. "There was an incident in the kitchen yesterday. There won't be a hot breakfast option today, but we have muffins available to grab over there."

"I don't eat carbs, unlike some people," Tiafel said. "I need my protein for breakfast."

"You're going to have to figure it out." My tone came out harsher than intended. I hadn't slept well, because I couldn't stop thinking about what Viridian had said. If I hadn't shirked my responsibilities for a day, the kitchen never would've been destroyed. The guilt kept me tossing and turning. Between that and my sore muscles, it was hard to be nice to someone like the fae.

Tiafel pressed her hands against the counter, her perfectly manicured nails clicking against the hard surface. "No, *you're* going to have to figure something out. You are the one who cooks food for me, and I have specific diet restraints, which means you have to accommodate me."

I opened my mouth, ready to snap at the beautiful fae, but a different voice filled the air.

"She's not your servant," Nyri said. "We are all here to help each other out, but I'm sure King Zathrian would *love* to hear how you're talking to Aukina, the one who feeds a hundred people every day."

Tiafel's lips puckered as if she had bitten into a lemon. "I don't understand why the demon king would date someone like you." Tiafel looked Nyri up and down, judgment pouring out of her eyes.

"What's that supposed to mean?" I asked. Tiafel had insulted my weight enough for me to know exactly what she was saying.

Nyri wasn't thin like the fae, but that didn't mean she was any less. She was stunning with her golden brown hair and dark blue eyes, and her curves outshone Tiafel's by mountains.

The fae pulled her lips into a taunting smile, and I braced myself for her harsh words. "It means that nobody wants to date people with a body like hers. Or like yours. There's no way the demon king would actually choose her unless he thought there was a way to use her."

Nyri's face faltered. Her relationship with the demon king had come as a surprise to Satella and me, especially since it was forbidden to speak with the demon king, but I saw the way he looked at her. That was what true love looked like.

"No," I said, pulling the fae's attention. "He would never date someone as cold and shallow as you. I don't get why land dwellers are so obsessed with thin bodies. In the ocean, women are considered beautiful for having curves. We don't discriminate for size. We see past the looks, which is how I know Nyri has a golden heart. It's no wonder the demon king fell for someone like her. Oh, and not everyone has the same biases as you, so stop tearing everyone else down. We are all at Ethlow for a reason and have our own demons. Stop making others miserable because of your insecurities."

Tiafel huffed. "Whatever. Neither of you are worth this." The fae stormed off.

I blinked several times, shocked by my own words. For years, she had thrown subtle insults at me, tearing apart my self-confidence bit by bit, and I had let her. The moment she insulted my friend, it was easy to bare my teeth.

"I didn't know you had that side to you," Nyri chuckled. She leaned her elbows against the counter, making her chest squeeze together. "Think you could get away from the kitchen for a bit? You look like you could use a breather."

The kitchen was clean, but after yesterday, I was afraid to step away. Nyri stared at me expectantly, as if she knew I was about to tell her no.

I chewed on my lip. A break didn't sound terrible. "Give me a few minutes, and I can join you for a bit."

I followed Nyri around the greenhouse, watching her touch plants with her magic, turning their color brighter in seconds. A few months ago, the building was a desolate graveyard, but under Nyri's guidance, it was filled with colorful plants and plentiful fruits and vegetables. It was incredible that she showed up at the demon king's estate not knowing she had magic in her bloodline, but she found a way to use it to help others. Her magic was in tune with plant life, making it grow when it was impossible under normal circumstances.

She stopped in front of the bleeding heart lily, gently touching its leaves. The flower wiggled under her touch, as if her presence brought it joy.

"I heard what happened in the kitchen from Zath," she finally said, revealing the truth behind our walk.

"Oh?" I didn't know what to say. I was sure Viridian had given a report to the king, who then told Nyri. It was strange to think my friend was dating one of the five demon rulers. The lands were ruled by demons, only one of the reasons my family discouraged mermaids to leave the sea. The water had different laws.

Before Nyri arrived, King Zathrian avoided the residents of Ethlow, so despite my five years at Ethlow, I hadn't met him until recently. Nyri and he fell into a whirlwind relationship that changed the estate for the better.

"Something about you spending the day away with a certain orange-haired guardsman, which led to a rat getting into the kitchen." She smiled knowingly.

"The kitchen was a disaster when I got back," I groaned. "I thought the place could function without me for one day, but apparently not. And what's Viridian's deal with rats? Isn't he some sort of powerful demon? Shouldn't he be able to incinerate a little rodent with his powers? Why did he destroy the place?"

Nyri placed her hands on her hips. "Uh-uh. You're not avoiding this. You spent the day with Reamann, and I heard a little rumor that you two were making out in the stables."

I groaned internally. I shouldn't have been surprised that rumors were already spreading about the two of us. Wistari was an incredibly hard worker, especially for her age, but she also loved gossip.

"We weren't making out in the stables. We barely kissed, and you knew about his surprise. He said you helped him out."

"I knew he wanted to surprise you, but I didn't know it was a date! You have to tell me everything. He kissed you? I've always thought you two would be cute together." Nyri couldn't stop gushing. She loved romance, whether it was for herself or others.

"Weren't you just saying how good you thought Ovid and I would be together?" Satella had teased me about Reamann before, but Nyri didn't tease as much as the vampire.

Nyri rolled her eyes. "He's a jerk, but Reamann is a good guy."

I was skeptical of Nyri's comments. It wasn't that long ago that she had cleared out the greenhouse in hopes of Ovid and me moving further into a relationship. "I never realized how sweet Reamann was." I bit my lip in an attempt to hide my smile.

Nyri's face softened, shifting from giddy to something more serious. "You really like him, don't you?"

I didn't know how it had happened so fast. A few days ago, I saw Reamann as nothing but a friend, but I could never go back to seeing him as only a friend, even if it made my life more difficult.

"I do," I admitted. "He says he likes me, too, but it's a little hard to believe. It feels like a crazy dream."

Nyri squealed, practically bouncing with excitement. "Ugh, you two are too cute. Now tell me everything that happened yesterday. I don't want you to leave out any details."

And so I did, and the more I told her about Reamann, the more I felt myself falling for the half-demon who reminded me what it was like to be free.

By the end of the day, the kitchen resembled the chaotic norm. Dishes needed to be replaced, but I had put an order in to the glassmakers and potters for those. The dinner rush finished, with only a few late residents lingering, so I had released Wistari and the others for the day, staying behind to make sure everything was in order.

My body begged me to stop for the night, but I couldn't get Viridian's comment out of my head. I had plenty of help in the kitchen, but there wasn't someone who could take over command when I wasn't there. Cibil used to run the kitchen seamlessly, so I thought leaving them in charge for a day would've been fine. But old age had caught up with the gnome. I wanted to prove Viridian wrong, to show him I could handle the responsibilities on my own, but I didn't know what to do.

"Still working?" Reamann leaned on the counter, poking his head through the gap in the wall.

His voice chased away my worries. "I'm almost done." I wiped a few more sections of the counter and organized ingredients for breakfast. Once done, I moved to the counter where Reamann patiently waited for me.

"You need to learn to relax and let others take control," the half-demon said.

I raised my eyebrows. "You saw what happened yesterday when I took a day off. You also heard what Master Viridian said about there being a problem."

"Viridian's right. There is a problem. You shouldn't have to work that hard every day to keep the kitchen running smoothly. Even guards get days off."

My chest tightened in defense. "I can handle it just fine." I turned away from him and walked to the other side of the kitchen. I wanted to prove to everyone that I didn't need help.

Reamann hopped over the counter, sliding into the kitchen. "There's nothing wrong with asking for help. You do so much for everyone. You deserve a break."

He was right, but it didn't stop the burning need to do everything. I leaned against the counter and crossed my arms. Reamann's eyes flicked lower, drawn to my chest. He forced himself to look back at me. Heat pooled between my legs. There was something about the desire in his eyes that made it difficult to think.

I dropped my arms and looked away from him, knowing I couldn't continue this conversation if I was looking at him. "Maybe I don't deserve a break."

"Everyone deserves a break."

Reamann didn't understand, and I wasn't sure how to change that without telling him exactly who I was. My past was something I kept close to my heart. I didn't want anyone to know the world I had run away from. I didn't want them to treat me differently because I wasn't born into a regular family.

I took a shallow breath. "People were relying on me in the Hallow Sea, and I ran away from my responsibilities. The least I can do is do my part in Ethlow." It was only a kernel of the truth, but I couldn't bring myself to say more.

Reamann grabbed my hips and pulled me closer to him. He pushed my hair out of my face before tracing my cheek and my neck. "I understand the guilt of running away, but you shouldn't punish yourself for it. You ran for a reason. You shouldn't suffer because of one decision you made."

"Maybe I deserve to suffer." I didn't want my old life. I had been engaged to a merman for political reasons, but I had wanted to find love. I wanted to find my own way in the world without my mother telling me how to dress and act.

"You, of all beings, don't deserve to suffer. You deserve to be happy and at peace. You deserve to enjoy your life and take breaks." He twisted his fingers in my hair, the sensation soothing and calming.

"I don't know how to do that," I whispered.

Reamann's lips curled into a smirk. "Let me help you." He lifted me onto the counter without warning, making me squeak. He spread my legs, settling himself between them as he pulled himself closer. His hand slid under my dress, tracing my calf and then my thigh. His fingers danced dangerously close to my core, making my breath hitch. I had never wanted someone to touch me there that desperately before. He leaned in and whispered, "Just relax and let me do all the work."

Chapter
10

I pressed my hands against his shoulders. "What if someone sees?"

Reamann traced my underwear, teasing my pussy with his fingers. The thin piece of cloth was the only thing separating us. "There's no one here."

The mess hall was empty, but someone could walk in on us. Despite knowing this, I spread my legs further, desperate for more. My heart thrummed, knowing we could get caught at any second, but I had never had anyone touch me like that—not in my human form. It was different with a tail.

It was better without a tail.

Reamann pressed his lips against the side of my neck, and a tingling sensation crawled over my skin, leaving goosebumps in its wake. A small moan filled the air, quickly followed by Reamann's chuckle. I tried to fight the embarrassment crawling up my neck and burning my cheeks.

"You are so beautiful," Reamann muttered against my neck.

His words felt hard to believe, but that wasn't always the case. In the Hallow Sea, I was considered stunning, but my time away from merfolk had twisted my view of beauty. But as Reamann continued kissing my neck and teasing my pussy with his fingers, it was hard to deny. If the half-demon didn't think I was beautiful, he wouldn't have wasted his time on me.

"Reamann." Nerves pricked my skin. I wanted him to keep touching me, but part of me was afraid that once he got a taste of me, he'd disappear.

His red eyes found mine, our breaths mingling. "Are you okay?" Such soft, caring words. It was enough to remind me that I was safe with him. He wasn't going to call me a whale or unlovable.

"It's just..." I bit my lower lip, too embarrassed to say it out loud. "It's been awhile since, um..."

Reamann furrowed his eyebrows, trying to figure out what I was trying to say. I wanted to smack my forehead for being too vague, but it was hard to say out loud. I was afraid that once Reamann knew I had limited experience in this form, he would think there was something wrong with me.

I lowered my voice, knowing there was no way around it. "I haven't had sex since leaving the Hallow Sea, and I've never had it with legs." There it was. It wasn't exactly a secret, but I couldn't stop the shame from pooling in my chest. It had been over six years since the last time I had done anything with the male species, and it felt as if I had forgotten everything.

"Ah." Recognition flooded his face, and I waited for him to pull away. "Then let me make it worth the wait." He paused, a question in his eyes. He didn't want to do anything until he received permission from me.

"Okay," I whispered. My heart raced with anticipation.

Reamann hooked his fingers on the side of my underwear and pulled them down until they dropped to the floor. He pushed my dress higher, exposing my thighs. His fingers lightly traced my inner thighs, taking his time to move between my legs. I spread my legs as far as they could go, urging him to continue. There was an ache in my core that burned with a new passion. I had craved being held and kissed and loved, but this was lust and desire.

Reamann kept his eyes on mine as he dipped his fingers between my legs. He moved up and down, carefully coating his fingers in my arousal. I couldn't slow my breathing, too focused on every little touch he made, fear and excitement spun together in a tangle of webs. When he found the little bundle of nerves, he moved around it in slow circles. My heart rate sped as pleasure spread throughout the rest of my body. Anyone could walk in on us, but that made every touch more exciting.

My eyes fluttered shut as I took in the new sensations. Reamann cupped my cheek and pulled me into a kiss. He ran his tongue over my lips, and I parted my mouth, giving him full access. He slipped his tongue inside, dancing with the tip of mine. I moaned again, unable to contain myself. My body was flushed and warm, but I didn't care. I wanted more.

I grabbed the back of his head, desperate for him to be closer. The different sensations clouded my thoughts, and I needed to hold onto the demon in front of me to stop myself from losing myself completely. His hair was soft beneath my fingers, and as I tugged on it, he groaned, sending a shock of excitement through my spine. I wanted to hear him make all sorts of noises.

Reamann pushed a finger into my entrance, and a small whimper escaped my mouth. He broke the kiss and asked, "Are you okay?"

I nodded quickly. I was more than okay, but the way he checked on me made me feel safe. "Don't stop." It was a soft plea compared to the desperation I felt inside.

He didn't hesitate to follow my instructions. He moved his finger in and out of me, curling up and hitting a spot that made my body quiver. His lips found my neck, and he sucked and nipped at my sensitive skin, moving down slowly. He took his time at my collarbone, and I stretched my neck to the side to give him better access. He scraped his teeth against my skin. Every touch from him was gentle and calculated.

It felt incredible, but there was a small part of me that wondered what it'd be like for him to lose control, to be a little rougher. I wanted him to take every part of me like I was everything he ever needed.

Reamann slipped a second finger inside me, and my breathing grew ragged. Pressure unlike anything I had experienced before filled my core. I clung to his neck, afraid I would shake uncontrollably if I let go of him.

He brushed his thumb over my clit as he continued to pump into me, and my entire body tensed. "Just relax," he whispered before kissing me again.

I melted into his touch, and the moment I let go of control, a crashing wave of pleasure rushed through me. My walls pulsed around his fingers, and he continued moving inside of me, causing additional waves to flood my system. Only when my body slumped with exhaustion did he stop. He pulled his hand out from between my legs and stuck his fingers into his mouth, cleaning my juices off his digits.

He hummed. "You taste better than I ever imagined."

I didn't know what to say, giddiness filling my chest. I was exhausted on ten different levels, but I couldn't stop beaming at the demon in front of me. I had never imagined *that* happening between us.

"How do you feel?" he asked, rubbing his thumb against my cheek.

"Wonderful," I said. "And tired."

He chuckled and kissed my forehead. "Good."

"Does it always feel like that?" I asked. It felt like a silly question, but as a mermaid, it felt different.

"It can, if your partner knows what he's doing." There was a slight cockiness to his tone that made me squeeze my legs shut. I had just gotten a taste of what he was capable of, which made my mind wander.

"Is it the same if you are in your demon form?" I hadn't seen Reamann at night. Even before he had been switched to the night shift, he was never around after dark. I hadn't thought anything about it before, but now I wanted to know what he looked like when his demon side came out.

Reamann tensed. "I don't know. I've never done it in my demon form."

"Maybe we could try." I didn't know what had gotten into me. A single taste had broken the seal on the door I had kept my desires behind, and I couldn't stop my thoughts from spinning out of control.

Reamann looked away from me. "That's not a good idea."

"Why not?" The fear of rejection festered in my chest.

He didn't respond right away, as if he was searching for the perfect words. "When my demon side comes out, I don't have as much control. The last thing I want to do is hurt you."

It was a struggle to imagine Reamann being able to hurt me in any way. He was careful and checked in to make sure I was okay. When he was with me, I felt safe in a way I never had felt before. But I didn't want to push him.

"Okay," was all I said, afraid he'd see through my disappointment if I said anything else.

"But next time we have a moment together, I want to taste every part of you." He gripped my thigh, making my need grow in an instant.

I pulled him into a kiss, needing to feel him against me to drown out any lingering disappointment.

Too soon, he broke the kiss. "I have to go, but I can walk you to your room before I go."

I didn't want him to leave, but he had responsibilities he couldn't ignore for me, just like I couldn't ignore the kitchen for him. "It's okay. There are a few more things I want to do here."

"Do you ever stop moving?"

"When I stop moving, and I'm alone, my thoughts get louder."
Thoughts of my family and the life I abandoned. Fears of rejection
and feelings of not being good enough. If I wasn't careful, it became a dark road, one I didn't share with anyone else.

"What kind of thoughts?" He was delaying leaving for his shift.
I didn't blame him, but I didn't want to get him in trouble.

"You should go." I didn't want to talk about the thoughts that
filled my head when there weren't distractions.

"Only if you promise to get some rest tonight."

"I promise." I kissed him again. He lifted me down with control
that came from his well-trained muscles.

He kissed me one last time. "I'll see you tomorrow, okay?"

"Okay." He hadn't left yet, but I felt myself missing him. I didn't
want him to leave so soon after what we did, but neither of us had
control over that. "Stay safe tonight."

Chapter

II

Nothing could ruin my mood. Days flew by in a magical whirl thanks to Reamann. We spent as much time together as possible—which wasn't much considering our opposite schedules, but the time we did spend together was mind-blowing.

"Someone is in love," Wistari said as she kneaded a batch of dough for bread.

I tore pieces of dough off my own batch and worked it into a log shape. For a moment, I didn't realize she had been talking to me, but the rest of the kitchen staff kept their noses in their work. "What are you talking about?"

"You haven't stopped smiling since I came in this morning," Wistari said. "Even when Tiafel came by, your mood didn't shift. It's Reamann, isn't it?"

I was sure the young elf was the one who spread the rumors about Reamann and I making out. "Maybe," was all I said. I wasn't ready for her to tell the estate I was in love, when everything was too new for me to understand.

Wistari giggled, clapping her dough-covered hands. "Oh, I've been hoping you'd wake up and realize you and Reamann were meant to be. He's liked you for like ever."

Was I the only one who hadn't realized Reamann liked me? I couldn't decide if I was that dense or if I had been blinded by my crush on a certain merchant. "Since when did you get so invested in my love life?"

Wistari was a fresh eighteen. She was no longer a child, but when she first arrived three years ago, she was. It was rare for Viridian to accept residents who were considered children. Many of the children who showed up were running away from a perfectly good life because they had gotten into an argument with their parents. He made exceptions for orphaned children who had nowhere else to go. Elcy, the resident teacher, took care of anyone who needed guidance.

"Since you spend all your free time in the kitchen, you need to learn to get a life outside this place." She put her hands on her hips, leaving flour handprints on her shirt. "You're not even in charge of the kitchen, yet you dedicate more time here than anyone else. But, now that you have a boyfriend, maybe you'll learn to delegate your time appropriately."

Wistari wasn't the first one who had said I spent too much time in the kitchen. Satella and Nyri had said something similar to me during our meal breaks. I didn't have any hobbies outside of cooking, but it hadn't felt like a problem before.

"The delivery is here!" one of the other kitchen staff called out.

My stomach twisted into seven different knots. I had been too distracted by the week to realize that today was the day Ovid was supposed to bring our supplies. For a moment, I debated about asking Wistari to accept the delivery on my behalf, but I didn't want to subject the young girl to the merchant after learning the truth about what kind of male he was.

I wiped my hands on a damp cloth and took a deep breath, steeling myself for the interaction that was to come.

Ovid was already outside, a frown carved into his face as he shielded his eyes from the sun. When he saw me, his expression brightened.

"Good morning, my beautiful flower," he purred, as if he hadn't called me a whale the week prior.

I faltered, unsure of what to do with his sudden attitude change. I had prepared myself for more insults. "Good morning." I kept my voice curt, uninterested in playing nice with the merchant.

"Don't be like that," He took a step towards me, making me flinch. "You know I didn't mean those things I said. I was just having a bad day. But I would love to go see the bleeding heart lily with you again. This time, I'll make it special."

I didn't know what to make of his mood. He was acting as if what he said to me wasn't a big deal, but I wasn't buying his act. He showed me his true colors, and I believed them. It wasn't just a bad day. "No, thank you."

"Oh, come on, my beautiful flower. I know you like me. Maybe we could go at a time when no one else is there, and I can show you a good time." He grabbed my hand and pressed his lips against it.

My insides recoiled at his touch. I pulled my hand away, taking a step back to create space. "Not interested, and don't touch me again. The only thing I'm interested in is the supplies you brought. Did you bring everything on my list?"

Ovid closed the distance between us and grabbed my chin. He towered over me, looking down at me with darkened eyes. "Don't be ungrateful. Someone like you should be thrilled that someone like me is willing to pay attention to you. If you behave like a good little girl and take me to the flower, then I can make you feel things no one else would bother to."

Disgust was an understatement for what I felt. "Get your hand off me now."

Ovid clicked his tongue and tightened his grip. "This is why no one will ever love you."

I swung my arm, hitting Ovid in the jaw with my fist. There was a sharp pain in my fingers, but he let go, giving me a chance to back away from him. He rubbed his jaw, his fury burning like a raging forest fire. I had to run. It was too dangerous to stay. I turned, taking off as fast as I could, but it wasn't fast enough. Ovid grabbed my arm and yanked me backwards.

"You ungrateful whale."

I thrashed, trying to force him to let go, but he dug his fingers into my skin.

"Let go!" I screamed as loudly as I could. I didn't know what Ovid was capable of, and I was scared to find out.

Heavy footsteps filled the air, but before I saw where they were coming from, I heard a *thwack*! Ovid let go of me and stumbled backwards.

"If you ever touch her again, I will kill you," Reamann growled. His eyes flared red as he squared up against the merchant.

"This is none of your business." Ovid stepped towards me, but he didn't get far.

Reamann grabbed his arm and twisted it behind his back. He slammed Ovid's head against the cart, and the merchant dropped to the ground, blood pouring from his hair.

Ovid curled his lip back as he looked up at Reamann, baring his canines. "You're going to regret that."

"I don't think I will." Reamann wasn't phased by the merchant's words. He didn't care what kind of repercussions came from the attack.

"What is going on here?" Viridian appeared from the shadows, his power filling the air and making it difficult to breathe. He looked between the three of us, his eyes narrowing. "Reamann, Aukina, go to the demon king's office immediately."

Ovid smirked, triumph filling his face. It made me want to punch him again, but I didn't dare do anything to the merchant with Viridian's anger in the way.

Chapter

12

I cradled my aching wrist, saying nothing as Reamann and I waited for the demon king to show up. The silence between us was unbearable, but I didn't know what to say. I stole a glance at the half-demon. He was fuming with clenched fists, and I couldn't tell if he was angry with me or Ovid.

Maybe both.

"Thank you," I whispered. It felt like I couldn't speak at a normal volume in the demon king's office. Even though Nyri was dating him, he felt beyond my level, and I hadn't had a normal conversation with the King of Kinzlea.

Reamann's eyes were fixated on the desk in front of him. The room had minimal decorations, and the desk was empty except for piles of paperwork.

"Why didn't you tell me what that merchant had said to you?" The bitterness in Reamann's voice made my heart ache. I wanted him to hold me to make the pain go away, but I didn't feel like I had the right to his comfort.

"I was embarrassed and afraid, and I thought I could handle it on my own. I didn't think he'd..." I had never been attacked like that before. I had believed Ovid was a good guy for years, wasting my time liking someone like him. It was embarrassing and foolish.

Reamann let out an exasperated sigh. "How can I prove to you that you don't have to do everything on your own? I want you to know you can rely on me. You can rely on Nyri and Satella, too. You don't always have to put on a brave face."

He was right, but I was afraid of becoming a burden. I ran away from a life others would have killed for. The last thing I deserved was to make other lives miserable just to ease my own burdens, but it was more than that.

"I know, but I didn't want you to know what he thought of me, because I was afraid that if you knew, it'd make you realize you were wasting time with me." I hated saying that out loud. I hated how far my confidence had crumbled over the years. Where was the strong woman who told her family no and fought for a different life? Where was the mermaid who was determined to live the kind of life she wanted?

"Look at me." His soft command pulled my eyes to his. "Nothing anyone else says about you will change my mind, especially not an arrogant merchant who thinks he's better than everyone else. You are incredible, Aukina. Nothing and no one can make me think otherwise."

I wanted to believe that, but part of me worried that if he knew the truth about who I was, he'd change his mind. It was time to get it over with, so he could make his decision before we got more wrapped up in each other. I opened my mouth, prepared to tell him about my secret past.

The door swung open, and Viridian walked into the room. His posture was stiff and composed, but there was a storm in his eyes, ready to rain down on us. He stepped behind the desk, but he didn't sit down. One hand rested on his abdomen, and his other hand was tucked behind him. Small shadows pricked at his aura, his anger simmering below.

"I don't usually get involved in the personal affairs of the residents at Ethlow," Viridian began. His words were laced with annoyance, and I settled in for the lecture that was sure to come. "But ever since the two of you began whatever it is you're doing, you have caused me more headaches than ever before. I thought switching Reamann to the night shift would be punishment enough to clear your heads, but it's only gotten worse."

I glanced at Reamann. He never told me his shift was switched as a punishment.

Viridian clicked his tongue, bringing my attention back to him. "Not only does the kitchen need repairs, but now I have to figure out what to do about the merchant."

I didn't dare tell the master of the house that he had caused the damage to the kitchen.

"We are going to find a new merchant to do business with," a deep voice rang from behind us. A new power filled the air, one that was strong with a touch of chaos. The hair on the back of my neck rose. I was trapped in a room with three demons, something I had never experienced before.

The demon king strode into the room and took a seat in his chair. He wore a black suit with a dark maroon jacket hanging over his shoulders, an outfit that looked like too much for the summer heat. The estate was cooled with magic, but it couldn't stop all the heat from the summer sun.

The demon king's horns curled out of his head, and his maroon hair twisted around them. He was only partially in his demon form, but it made him more intimidating. He intertwined his fingers and leaned forward. It was impossible to look away from him. His aura was commanding in every way. It was no wonder Nyri found herself wrapped up with a demon like that.

"Is your hand okay?" The demon king gestured towards me.

Bruising covered my knuckles, and I could barely move my fingers. I didn't want to tell that to one of the five most powerful demons in the land. "It... hurts."

He hummed, displeased by my answer or maybe by the situation. I couldn't tell. "Make sure to get it checked out as soon as we're done here. I already heard Viridian's account of what happened, but I want to hear it from your side."

I glanced at Reamann, but he was focused on my hand. It would've been easier to tell the whole story without Reamann present, but I didn't have a choice. "Last week, Ovid asked me to take him to see the bleeding heart lily, and I agreed. I thought... I thought maybe he liked me, but he had no interest in me, only the flower. Out of anger, I told him to leave, but he wasn't happy about it." It was strange thinking that only a week ago I had eyes for the merchant, especially now that I was wrapped up in Reamann's charms.

"She fell and hit her head during the incident," Reamann added. "Or he pushed her. I don't know which." His side glance made me wince. I had chalked up the incident to be an accident, but after what Reamann saw, I was sure he didn't believe that.

The demon king lifted his eyebrows, waiting for me to clarify.

There was no way out of this. "He grabbed me, so I stomped on his foot to make him let go. He pushed me, and I lost my balance, hitting my head as I fell."

The rage flowing off Reamann was comparable to the power of the two other demons in the room. "I should've killed him that day."

The demon king lifted his hand, silencing Reamann in a heartbeat. "And what happened today?"

"He wanted me to take him to see the flower again, and when I said no, he got aggressive. He wouldn't let go, so I punched him. It only worked for a moment, and I couldn't get away fast enough. He grabbed me again, and that's when Reamann stepped in. He protected me. He doesn't deserve to be punished for this. It's my fault." I hung my head in shame. I had only caused issues for others recently, and I didn't know how to stop the spiral from continuing.

"I'm not punishing anyone." The demon king's tone was kinder than I had expected, especially after the way Viridian had been speaking to us. "I wish you had come to me the first time the merchant touched you. I would've found someone else to do business with immediately."

"Really?" I hadn't said anything because I had been afraid it would've come down to my word against the merchant's.

Viridian straightened. "It is our priority to protect the residents of Ethlow against any outside force, including violent merchants. By not reporting this sooner, you've caused a headache for the sire and me. Next time, I expect you to tell me when you have any issues—like being overworked in the kitchen." His comment was pointed, making it feel like another scolding was in my future.

"Be nice to her," the demon king said. "We don't want the best cook we've ever had to leave us, now would we, Viridian?"

Viridian's face tightened. "No, sire. We wouldn't."

A compliment from the demon king. There was no higher praise than that. "Thank you so much Mr.—Sire—uh your majesty." I hadn't addressed him directly before in a formal situation and didn't know how to talk to him.

The demon king chuckled. "Please, call me Zathrian."

"I'd prefer it if she didn't," Viridian said.

The demon king hollered with laughter. "You're too uptight, Viridian. Maybe it's time for you to take a vacation."

"Yes, sire," Viridian answered, but it was clear he had no intention of taking a vacation. Ethlow was his life.

"You two are dismissed." The demon king turned to Reamann. "Make sure to take proper care of her."

Reamann bowed his head. "I will. Thank you, your majesty." He offered me his hand and helped me up, guiding me to the door.

I hesitated before stepping outside the office. "Thank you, Zathrian." It felt strange to address the demon king by his name, but a bright smile painted his face the moment I said it, making it feel like the right choice, even as Viridian glowered next to him.

"I don't think I've had someone need this much medical attention in such a short time frame," Satella said, carefully inspecting my wrist and fingers. Reamann sat on the other side of the room, waiting for the vampire to finish her inspection. "You've never been this prone to accidents before."

"It's that merchant's fault," Reamann muttered, his arms crossed. "If I ever see him again, I will kill him."

"This is why I hate males," Satella said. "They think they can treat women however they want."

"Excuse me. I'm a male," Reamann said.

Satella narrowed her eyes. "And?"

"You say that like it's a bad thing."

"Prove to me it's not by treating Aukina right, then." Satella could tell Reamann was annoyed with her, but that didn't stop her from pushing.

"I swear to you, I will make sure that merchant doesn't lay another hand on her. I will keep her safe." The intensity in Reamann's eyes made my insides quiver. No one had defended me like he did, and it made my body ache for him.

"Woof," Satella said. She wiggled her eyebrows and said under her breath, "You have some scary dog privilege."

My thighs clenched, knowing she was right. The anger oozing off Reamann was new and strange. If he hadn't stepped in today, I didn't know what would've happened, and thinking about the fury he had the moment he saw Ovid's hands on me made my blood boil. "It's kind of nice."

"What are you two whispering about over there?" Reamann asked.

"Just about how you better not fuck things up with Aukina," Satella said, sending a wink in my direction. Reamann glared at her, and she made a vulgar gesture in return. Then she whispered, "It seems like you have a good one."

"Yeah," I agreed. I smiled at Reamann, and he smiled back.

Satella quickly finished wrapping my hand, telling me I couldn't use it for the next week or so. When she was done, Reamann walked me to my room. We were both silent, but it was different from the walk to the demon king's office. When we reached my door, I lingered outside, not ready to say goodbye.

I leaned against the wall. "I didn't get a chance to thank you for stepping in today."

Reamann pressed his hand against the wall above my head and leaned in. His body surrounded me like a shield, making me feel safe, despite the lingering terror from Ovid's attack. "If you ever have a problem, or someone is hurting you, please tell me. I will make sure they never touch you again." The intensity in his eyes made my heart stutter. Reamann would kill for me, and there was something about that thought that cracked my chest open.

My instinct was to tell him that I could handle myself, but the situation with Ovid proved otherwise. Maybe it was time for me to start leaning on others. "I will."

"Good." He brushed his nose against mine, teasing me before tasting my lips. He moved slowly, as if he was afraid I was going to break.

"I'm okay." I wasn't sure which one of us needed to hear that more.

"I know." He kissed me again. I grabbed his shirt with my good hand, stopping him from pulling away.

"Don't go." It was a plea. After the way Ovid attacked me, I didn't want to be alone.

"I need to get some sleep before tonight, or I'll be useless." The apprehension in his voice told me he didn't want to go. It was only fair to let him sleep, since he had to stay awake all night, but I didn't want to be alone.

"Then sleep in my bed. I won't bother you. I could use the company." I prepared myself for his rejection, telling myself it was okay if he said no.

Reamann buried his face in the crook of my neck. "It's impossible to say no to you."

"You don't have to if—"

"No," he interrupted. He picked me up, being careful of my injured hand. "I'm not going anywhere."

Chapter 13

Not being able to use my dominant hand in the kitchen was a punishment. I tried to help prepare food, but Wistari and the others told me to go relax. I stayed and helped where I could.

"You should just go and rest," Wistari said, snatching a whisk from me.

"I can help," I said for the umpteenth time.

"Do I have to chase you out of the kitchen?" Despite the elf's young age, she had a commanding aura that would bring men to their knees.

"Don't worry. I'll whisk her away," Nyri said, poking her head into the kitchen. Wistari gave her a grateful smile.

"Let me just grab some food for us," I said.

"Aren't you supposed to be resting to heal your hand?" Nyri swept past me and took the plates of food out of my hands.

"The bone is only fractured, not broken. With Satella's salves, she said it'd heal in a week."

"*If* you rest." I tried to ignore Nyri's pointed look. She didn't understand my need to keep moving. I feared the kitchen would fall apart without me if I took a week off.

"I'm being careful." I tried to take the plates back, but Nyri easily twisted away from me.

"She's not," Wistari called out, earning me a dirty look from Nyri.

"I'll be outside, but if you need anything, come get me," I told the young elf, ignoring her comment.

"I won't need you. We can finish the prep for dinner just fine."

I hesitated, hating to leave the kitchen, but Nyri was waiting for me. I followed her outside to the abandoned courtyard that had become our eating place. Satella was already there, stretched out in the sun, taking in all the heat. Looking at her made me queasy. I didn't understand how she did it. Vampires were more prone to heat exhaustion than mermaids, yet she acted as if it gave her energy.

I opted to sit in the shade, knowing my body didn't handle heat well, since it was used to the icy waters of the Hallow Sea.

"When I said take it easy, I meant no kitchen work," Satella said, taking her bowl of soup and setting it to the side. She rarely ate with us, since her diet consisted mostly of blood. The only time she ate with us was when I made soup, and even then, sometimes the vampire opted out of her favorite food.

"You already knew that wasn't going to happen," I said. Satella and I had been friends long enough that she knew I rarely stopped to breathe. She had suggested I slow down at the beginning of our friendship, but she stopped mentioning it years ago.

"If you reinjure it, I'm not going to help you."

I shook my head at the vampire. "You know that's not true."

She pursed her lips, annoyance taking over her features. She knew I was right. She never turned down a soul in need.

"You two are ridiculous," Nyri said, smiling. She always enjoyed the banter between Satella and me. When she came to the estate, she had no one, which I struggled to understand. She was sweet and kind. The world had been harsh on the human girl. It was easy to adopt her into our makeshift family.

"You love it," I said.

"Yeah." Nyri chuckled. "So are you okay, Aukina? I mean, other than your hand."

Her question threw me off. I was fine, at least that was what I had told everyone. It wasn't false, but it wasn't true, either. Ovid grabbing me like that had shaken me up. At the moment, I hadn't known what he was capable of, which was the scariest part.

"I'm...managing."

Satella sat up, her attention drawn to me. "That must've been pretty scary to have him attack you like that."

It wasn't scary. Scary was running away from home, leaving everything I knew for a world that was a mystery to me. What Ovid did had left a terror behind that sank into my bones, one that haunted me every second I had to think. "I'm just glad Reamann showed up when he did."

"A knight in shining armor," Nyri cooed. "Or should I say a demon in shining armor?"

Before leaving the Hallow Seas, I hadn't met a demon before. Growing up, I thought demons were selfish and evil. Reamann was nothing like that.

I pulled my knees to my chest, not feeling particularly hungry. "I keep thinking what would've happened if Reamann hadn't shown up when he did." A shudder ran through my spine, and the mood dropped. "What I don't understand is why Ovid kept asking me to take him to the flower. He got so angry when I told him no. He could've seen it without me, so why bother me?"

"Actually, he couldn't," Nyri said. "The greenhouse is off limits to non-residents. Without an escort, Ovid couldn't see the flower."

"But why was he so obsessed with it?" On the Nescen Islands, the bleeding heart lilies were considered magical flowers. Couples went to see them, because it was said to bring them luck. Ovid had no interest in dating me.

"Bleeding heart lilies are worth a fortune on land," Nyri said. "The only reason I got my hands on one is because of Zathrian, and I'm afraid to ask what it cost him. The flower is considered not only rare, but it is said to have magical elements. Witches have theorized that they have magical healing abilities, but the flowers are too rare for them to experiment with. He was probably obsessed with it because he's a merchant. He knows exactly what it's worth."

My stomach twisted. "So he was trying to use me to steal the flower?"

Nyri shrugged. "It would have been stupid for him to try to steal from the demon king's estate."

"Males are stupid," Satella chimed in. She was right, and it left me with an uneasy feeling.

Ↄↄ

With each day that passed, the mobility in my fingers increased, but Satella told me I had to keep my hand wrapped for several more days. If I moved it the wrong way, it could reinjure my hand. It was frustrating, but I told myself it was only a few more days.

I wiped down the counters and cleaned the kitchen after the dinner rush. Despite the frustration of not being able to cook, I found myself smiling, knowing Reamann would swing by soon to say hi before his shift. He had been making a point to check in after he was released for the night before breakfast, and again after he slept.

Clouds thickened in the sky, blocking the sun and making it nearly impossible to tell the time. It was supposed to rain for the next few days, which wasn't surprising. The summer had reached the point where storms happened almost weekly, leaving it muggy on top of warm. I didn't mind the wet air, but the rain meant days trapped inside. Before, I didn't mind the excuse to stay inside, but it was different now that Reamann and I were something.

"Do you need any more help here?" Wistari asked. She was one of the few that arrived before others and stayed late. I was the only one that spent more time in the kitchen than the young elf.

"No, I'm almost done," I said. I preferred to release her for the day before Reamann showed up. It gave us more privacy.

"Don't stay too late," Wistari said.

"I won't," I lied.

The young girl slipped out of the room, but it was only a moment later before she popped her head back inside. "Hey, Aukina?"

I hummed in response, barely glancing at the girl as I wiped the counter with my non-dominant hand.

"Were you expecting a delivery tonight?"

I left the rag on the counter and turned to the elf. "No?" It was a strange question for her to ask, especially at that time of day.

She scratched the back of her head, messing up the carefully placed braids decorating her hair. She had to spend at least an hour on her hair every day, if not more. "There's a cart outside. It kind of looks like Ovid's, but I know we stopped doing business with him." The nervousness in her voice put me on edge. She knew exactly what the merchant's cart looked like, and she wouldn't have brought it up casually.

"Show me." I followed her out through the exit. We didn't have to walk for long before the merchant's cart was visible. It looked like any normal cart, but it had blue-stained wheels. There was no doubt that it was Ovid's cart, but he had no reason to be there.

Unless...

"Wistari, I need you to find Reamann." The urgency in my voice made Wistari tense.

"Why?" She kept her feet planted. "What are you going to do?"

"I think Ovid is here to steal the bleeding heart lily. I need you to find Reamann and tell him I need him at the greenhouse immediately. Then tell Master Viridian. Understood?" My heart slammed against my chest, unable to get Nyri's words out of my head. If Ovid was here to steal the flower, sunset was the perfect time. It was against the rules to go outside at night, so by sunset, all residents returned to the estate, leaving the greenhouse empty.

Wistari grabbed my sleeve, as if she could read my mind. "It's almost dark. Let's find Reamann and Viridian together."

"It might be too late by the time we find them." I pulled out of the young girl's grip. "Don't worry. I'm just going to check on the flower. I'll be quick, and if he is there, I won't engage." All I had to do was distract him long enough for others to show up.

Wistari looked up at the clouds, but she couldn't tell the time any better than I could.

"Go," I ordered, mustering up as much authority as possible. She took a step back, hesitating a moment. Then she turned and ran.

And so did I.

I didn't know what I was doing. It was stupid to go to the greenhouse alone, but it was impossible to know how long Ovid had been there. It might've been too late already, but if there was any chance I could stop him from taking the flower that had become Nyri's proudest accomplishment, I had to try.

Thunder rolled over the land. It wasn't raining yet, but the clouds swirled with darkness. It wasn't long before they'd burst at the seams, letting water crash into the ground. I couldn't afford to get caught in the rain, but I couldn't stop.

A flash of lightning pulled my attention to the sky. *Caw!* A crow flew above me, as if it was following me to the greenhouse. The summer had been filled with crows, which was new. Crows had never dared to come to the demon king's estate until this year. Until Nyri showed up in the spring. They were harmless, so no one seemed to care about the sudden presence of the birds.

Thunder told me the storm was getting closer. My chest ached by the time I saw the glass panels of the greenhouse. I had never been a good runner. Between spending most of my childhood in the sea and having extra weight on my body, my lungs struggled to keep up. I refused to slow down until I stood in the door of the greenhouse. I grabbed the threshold as I struggled to catch my breath.

Ovid stood in the middle of the room, holding a shovel as he stood next to the bleeding heart lily. I had to do something to delay him long enough for others to show up. If I failed, he'd take the flower and all of Nyri's hard work with him.

Chapter 14

"Don't." My voice shook, and I didn't dare take another step forward.

Ovid paused, looking at me with darkened eyes. Any of the false pretenses he had before were gone. It made my heart twinge. How had I ever fallen for someone like him?

"Are you stalking me?" He kept one hand close to the flower. It wouldn't take much for him to destroy it. One wrong move, and I'd make everything worse.

"You're here to steal the bleeding heart lily." Memories of his hands on me made my body shake, but I refused to back down. Reamann and Viridian would show up soon. I only had to distract the merchant until they arrived.

"If you know what's good for you, you'll turn around and pretend like you saw nothing, unless you want to see my bad side." Ovid's blue eyes looked nothing like the piercing ocean I had remembered them as. Now that I knew his personality, his looks twisted into an ugly mask reflecting his soul.

"Reamann will be here any moment, and he'll stop you." I hoped Wistari found Reamann quickly, and he was already making his way to the greenhouse.

"If he shows up, I won't hesitate to kill that precious guard of yours." Ovid's eye was surrounded with a deep purple bruise from Reamann's attack.

"You're no match for him. He already proved that to you." And Reamann would prove it again the moment he showed up, not holding back a second time. I glanced outside, hoping to catch a glimpse of the orange-haired demon. There was nothing but the trees swaying in the wind of the approaching storm. Lightning flashed, quickly followed by thunder. The storm was nearly upon us.

"You're as stupid as you are ugly. Did you really think I'd come here unprepared against demons? If any of them come close, I have iron powder to dull their senses, and other weapons to kill them with." Ovid patted his satchel.

The thought of him hurting Reamann in any way replaced some of my fear with rage.

"Iron powder won't do anything against a demon. That's a myth." I didn't know if it was true, but I spoke as if it was. I had heard all the rumors about iron weakening demons enough to kill them, but I had never ventured to find out if it was true. I had no reason to discover a demon's weakness—not when I was living under the protection of one of the five great demons.

Ovid hesitated, doubt casting a shadow upon his face. "You're lying."

"Why don't you stick around and find out? The guardsmen are on their way to detain you now." I hoped that one wasn't a bluff.

Ovid muttered a curse under his breath. "Then I don't have time to deal with you." He stabbed the shovel into the dirt, digging the flower out by the roots.

"No!" I screamed, taking several steps forward. Instead of delaying him, I made him panic and rush.

Ovid pulled out a knife and pointed it at me. "Take another step, and this won't end well for you."

I froze, not daring to tempt the crooked male. "Please, stop. If you take the flower away from here, it'll die." Bleeding heart lilies had once grown in abundance on the Nescen Islands, but that was because the island had many skilled enough to handle the flower. Not only did Ovid know nothing about the flower, the dry weather of Kinzlea would kill the flower in days, if not sooner. I couldn't stand the thought of Nyri's hard work disappearing like that.

"The dead flower is more than enough to pay for my retirement. No more dealing with entitled royals demanding specific items, because I will be rich. You know, you can thank yourself for this. If you hadn't gotten me fired, I wouldn't have had to resort to thievery." Ovid was trying to push the blame onto me, and it partially worked. If I hadn't been in love with the idea of a man I knew nothing about, then I wouldn't have accepted his offer to go see the bleeding heart lily, and it wouldn't have devolved into what it did.

It would've been easy to let my mind spiral down that path, but I stopped it, knowing the merchant's words were nothing more than a distraction.

"You planned to steal the flower long before you got yourself fired. You're greedy, and I should've seen that sooner."

"So what if I'm greedy? This world takes and takes, crushing everyone it possibly can. You work in a mansion filled with desolate beings who have nowhere else to go. You should know exactly how cruel this world is and why I'm doing what I am." For a moment, I felt sorry for the merchant. I didn't understand what made him have such a dark look on the world, but it didn't matter. He was talking to the wrong person.

"I chose to walk away from my old life. Not everyone has that same fortune, but we work hard. We fight against cruelty. We don't add to it. You can choose a similar path. Don't do this. Walk away now." There was too much distance between us for me to hope to stop Ovid physically—not that I was brave enough to try. My only hope of stopping him was reaching a part of his heart that hadn't been blackened.

Ovid hesitated, as if contemplating my words. "No, thanks." He ripped the flower out of the dirt, and a cry escaped my mouth.

It wasn't too late. If Reamann or Viridian showed up soon, they could stop the merchant. Nyri could replant the flower. With her magic, it'd be saved. "I won't let you leave." My voice shook, my confidence abandoning me. I wasn't a match for the merchant. He had proved that twice already.

Ovid shoved the flower into his bag, damaging the delicate flower in the process. He pointed the knife at me again. "Either you can move, or I'll cut you down. Consider this me being nice and grateful."

I took a step to the side and lifted my hands, knowing there was only one choice. There was still time for others to show up, but my hope was dwindling.

"Maybe you're not totally helpless." He walked towards the door, keeping his eyes on me the entire time with the knife pointed at me. When he was nearly at the exit, he dug into his bag and pulled out a rope. "Tie yourself up." He tossed the rope at me, and it landed at my feet.

"What?"

"You heard me. Do it now, and do it quickly. I don't want you following me." Thunder cracked down, and sweat collected on the back of my neck from the humidity pooling in the air.

I grabbed the rope, my heart pounding. If I took my time, I'd buy the others a few more seconds. I didn't understand what was taking them so long. Maybe Wistari couldn't find them. Maybe they weren't coming at all, which meant I was on my own with the day ending and a storm coming. I should've listened to Wistari and not gone after Ovid. There was nothing I could do to stop him, but I wanted to believe I could slow him down enough for help to arrive.

"Hurry," he snapped, waving the knife at me.

My breath grew shallow at the thought of him coming at me with the knife. I wrapped the rope around my wrists. I knew exactly how to tie knots from the fisherman I had spent time with on the Nescen Islands. I held my hands up to show the merchant I had completed his order.

"Artagatis will find you and rain her karma upon your pathetic life," I said, rage filling every syllable.

"Guess it's a good thing I don't believe in gods and goddesses," Ovid said. "Don't try to come after me, or I won't hesitate to kill you." The merchant slipped out of the greenhouse.

I failed.

Lightning flashed, and thunder rolled. The sky quickly darkened. I wasn't sure if it was from the storm getting worse or the day nearly ending. Either way, I had to get back to the estate before it was too late. I waited for Ovid's body to disappear before I slipped my hands out of the fabricated restraints. He was a fool if he thought I'd properly tie myself up.

I rushed out of the building, glancing up at the sky. It wasn't raining yet, but that wouldn't hold true for much longer. I took off in a sprint, but I had hardly recovered from the run to the greenhouse. I was slower, and each step was harder than the last. The crashing thunder pushed me to continue, despite my body's protest. I couldn't get caught in the storm.

Caw!

I glanced up, surprised to find the same crow following me as before—at least I thought it was the same crow. They all looked the same, making it difficult to differentiate between the birds.

Caw! It felt as if the bird was taunting me, saying I wasn't going to make it in time. I wanted to scream at it, telling it to mind its own business, but yelling at a bird was ridiculous.

Small droplets of water hit my skin, but I didn't dare slow down. A little rain was fine, but if it picked up its pace, or I took too long to make it back to the estate, I'd get caught in the middle of the forest.

Caw! That call sounded like, *Stop!* But that was impossible. Birds couldn't speak.

I had to move faster, but I had already pushed my body past its limits. My lungs struggled. I hated my body on land. It was too heavy, which made it difficult to move the way I wanted to. In the water, I was faster than a crackling sailfish on a clear day.

The crow swooped down in front of me. I barely slowed down enough to avoid the attack.

"What do you want?" I screamed, frustration building in my core. My voice was drowned out by the increasing rain. I wasn't going to make it back to the estate.

The bird landed directly in front of me. Its beady eyes stared into my soul. There was a ring in its mouth with an orange gem. It dropped the ring and jumped into the sky, disappearing into the trees. I didn't have time to deal with a small trinket, but as I took a step away, an orange light flashed in the corner of my eyes. I hesitated, looking back at the ring that blended in with the dirt and leaves leftover from winter.

I was imagining things. I took another step, but a gnawing feeling in my gut made me turn back. I picked up the ring, but I didn't have any pockets to put it in, so I slid it on my finger as I took off again.

The rain came down harder, and it soaked through my clothes. I couldn't see the building through the trees, and the sky darkened. Lightning flashed, blinding me, and then my feet disappeared. I crashed to the ground, my hands scraping against the rough forest floor and my injured wrist screaming in pain. I rolled onto my back and wiped the water from my eyes, but it didn't do much with the constant downfall of water.

I flipped my tail, and my body shook. "No, no, no, no."

I was in the middle of the forest, the sky darkening at an alarming rate. With my fin, it was impossible to get back to the estate. There was nothing and no one around me to help. I had to find a way to get my legs back. It was the only way to make it out of the forest. I flipped back over and used my elbows to drag my body under a tree, hoping it provided enough protection from the rain to dry my body. The forest floor turned muddy as I crawled through it.

It was a lifetime before I made it to the trunk, and the sky had lost all light. The leaves blocked out some of the rain, but large drips found their way to my head, ensuring my hair was thoroughly soaked. I ripped my skirt off, knowing I'd never get dry enough with the soaked fabric clinging to my body. Leaning against the tree trunk, I closed my eyes.

It felt like the day I ran away from home. I swam nonstop until I reached the shores far away from the Hallow Seas. I had pulled myself onto the land and waited for the air to dry my skin enough to exchange my fins for legs. It was the loneliest I had ever felt, knowing I had no one and nowhere to go.

I had created a life in Ethlow. I made friends, and I had Reamann. But I was alone in the forest, afraid I'd never see the light of day again. It made me wonder what my life would've been like if I had just stayed in the Hallow Sea and followed the plan my parents had made for me. Maybe I would've found a way to be happy. I would've been safe. I had no doubt about that. Everything about my old life was safe.

Thunder roared in my ears, deafening my thoughts.

No.

That wasn't thunder.

A shadow flickered through the trees. The hair on the back of my neck stood on end. I wasn't alone. I held still, hardly breathing as I looked for more signs of movement. The dark wasn't an issue for my eyes. Mermaids swam in the depths of the ocean where light didn't reach. A forest on a stormy night was nothing for my night vision.

The animals had scurried to find shelter in the storm, leaving me alone. I couldn't see anything unusual, but I felt a presence, and it wasn't friendly. I couldn't run or fight. I was a fish out of water at the mercy of whatever beast hunted me.

Except, I wasn't one to back down. I grabbed a stick from the ground and held it, ignoring the sting in my cut-up palm. Dangerous creatures lurked around the demon king's estate at night. That was the reason rule two was created. From what I had learned over my time spent at Ethlow, the darkness opened windows from the netherworld where creatures crawled out of the depths of hell. The veil was the thinnest near powerful demons. Zathrian put up charms to protect the estate, but those protections didn't extend past the walls at night.

A branch snapped, and I flicked my head towards it. I blanched as I stared at a faceless creature. It had at least a dozen legs that held up a rounded body covered in spikes. There was a mouth that opened into a thousand sharp teeth. Death emanated from the creature in every way, from its aura to its stench.

A scream bubbled up from my chest, threatening to take over, but any sound could alert the creature to my presence. It had no eyes, which meant it relied on sound and vibration to hunt its prey. My hand shook as I stared at my own death, inches away from me.

I wasn't ready to die.

There was so much I wanted to do.

"Kina!" Reamann's voice echoed from close by.

My heart dropped as the creature turned towards the call of the demon. A rumble of clicks tumbled out of the creature's mouth, mixing with the rain and thunder.

"Kina! Where are you?" His voice was muffled by the rain, but he was near, and the creature knew it.

It took off, stabbing its sharpened legs into the ground. A flash of lightning revealed the silhouette of Reamann with a creature barreling towards him. All sense of self-preservation disappeared.

"Reamann!" I screamed.

The creature stopped and turned. It was closer to me, and I had just given away my location. It rushed towards me, the clicks drowning out every other sound as it prepared to pounce.

Chapter
15

I rolled through the dirt, barely moving in time for the creature to miss me. It barreled into the tree, and a crack as loud as thunder resounded in my ears. It stumbled back, dazed. I dug my elbows into the ground and dragged myself through the mud, but it was impossible to move fast. The creature turned its attention back to me, lifting one of its front legs. The razor sharp tip slammed into the ground next to my head, cutting a piece of my hair.

It lifted its leg up again, prepared to skewer me. I couldn't move, trapped by my own body. The creature swiped its two front legs, ready to split me open, but they never reached me. Reamann dove in front of it, blocking my body with his. His strong arms wrapped around my torso and tail as he picked me up in a fluid motion.

Before the creature attacked again, Reamann took off in a sprint. He cradled me in his arms, holding me close to his body. His eyes glowed bright red, like a beacon in the dark of the night. That was the only part of him that looked the same. Two thick horns twisted out of his head, pointing forward. His skin looked like charcoal with streams of lava flowing between the cracks. Sharp teeth filled his mouth as he clenched his jaw, running faster than mortally possible.

The clicking of the creature faded into the distance, but Reamann didn't slow down.

"We have to get back to the estate," I said, clutching his arm. The thought of that thing chasing us down made me want to cry.

"We can't." Reamann's voice was rougher than usual. "The wards are up, and if we lead that thing to the others, it will put the estate in danger."

I tightened my grip. I couldn't stand the thought of staying outside all night. "What about the barracks?" The barracks were separated from the rest of the estate. The guards spent their shifts there, which meant there'd be help.

"No." Reamann's voice was firm, and I didn't argue. "Don't worry. I know where to go." He tightened his grip and continued running. I didn't pay attention to where we were going, more focused on the clicks that faded behind us.

He didn't slow down until we reached an unfamiliar building. The door creaked from lack of use, and the smell of dust filled the air, but it was dry. The room was filled with wooden crates that had begun collecting cobwebs. Reamann set me on the closet one before going back to the door. He placed a metal bar over the wood, locking it from the inside.

He waited by the entrance, listening for signs of the creature. The wind hollowed outside, and when a crack of thunder crashed through the air, I flinched. There were no clicking sounds belonging to the creature, but Reamann waited another moment to be sure. Once he was satisfied, he turned to me, but he kept distance between us.

"We should be safe here for the night, but we can't make a fire, so it'll be cold." His voice was firm and calculated, not a drop of the sweet Reamann I knew.

"I don't really get cold," I said. Many thought mermaids were cold-blooded, but it was the opposite. Our blood was warmer than most other beings, making it easy to thrive in the cold ocean waters.

Reamann nodded. "Are you injured?"

"Nothing serious." The space between us felt unusually stale, and I hated it. If I had my legs, I would've rushed over to him, but I was stuck on the crate as long as my mermaid tail held me captive. "Are you injured?"

"I'll be fine." That wasn't a proper answer.

"Come here." I tried to sound commanding, but I couldn't hide the shake in my voice.

His body tensed, and he ignored my request. "Why did you leave the estate? You knew it was almost dark."

I swallowed, my throat tightening. I knew I had messed up, and Reamann's frustration only made it worse. "I thought I could help. I thought if I could delay Ovid long enough, either you or Viridian would show up and save the day."

"Damn it, Aukina. How could you be so stupid?" His fist hit the wall, making it shake beneath his fury.

The Reamann I knew had never spoken to me like that before. He was the sweetest and kindest man I had met.

"I was trying to be useful for once." My voice was as cold as the sea I was born in. I had messed up, but I didn't need him to yell at me because of it.

"You could've died. Do you not realize that?" He turned, his eyes flaring like burning rubies. His anger turned the air thick, and I couldn't stand it.

"I know." My voice cracked, all the fear I had pushed down in order to survive bubbled to the surface. I fought back against it. I couldn't fall apart. Not yet. Not with the tension pushing Reamann away from me. "What do you want me to say?"

His breath was heavy in the stale air. The cracks in his skin glowed, as if lava flowed beneath the surface of his skin. "It doesn't matter because it's too late."

His words were deafening. "What do you mean it's too late?" My mind went to the worst-case scenario. Was this the moment that Reamann realized I wasn't enough for him?

"You were never supposed to see me this way." He stretched his arms wide, showing the extra layers of muscle that belonged to his demon form. Lightning flashed, illuminating his mouth full of sharp teeth. His power radiated from him, a taste of death buried by ash and coal.

I couldn't look away from him. I hardly recognized the orange-haired man that had stolen my heart. Even his eyes glowed and moved with a force that would've scared me the day I stepped onto land.

I wasn't the same woman who left her home nearly six years ago. There were worse things in the world than demons.

"Why?" I asked.

"Because I'm a monster." Grit threaded his voice, making him sound different. "Because no one could love a demon like me. I destroy everything I touch."

"You are the furthest thing from a monster that I know." My heart cracked open. I needed to go to him, to close the distance between us. He hardly looked and sounded like the man I knew, but that didn't scare me.

When he didn't respond, I dug deep down and commanded with the authority of a royal, "Come here."

Reamann dropped his arms, but he didn't move. "I don't want to hurt you."

I needed to show him I wasn't afraid of him. "You won't."

He didn't move, which meant I had to go to him. I rang out my hair, trying to dry my body enough for my legs to return.

"Maybe this was a mistake," he whispered. "I shouldn't have pursued you, knowing there was this side to me." Reamann's head hung low, and I felt him slipping away from me.

Fear worse than facing Ovid or that creature slammed into my chest. I had never been so desperate to shed my fins for legs. I hated my mermaid side deeper than I ever had before. I stripped my shirt, desperate to make my skin dry.

"Reamann, look at me."

He didn't listen, and I could hardly breathe. I needed to get to him to show him that he was wrong. I was ready to push myself off the crate and crawl across the ground in my mermaid form, but then my tail split into two legs. I had never been more grateful to feel human.

I hopped off the crate and ran to the demon. He towered over me in his demon form, but I didn't care. I lifted onto my toes and grabbed his face. "I have made countless mistakes in my life, but falling for you is not one of them."

Reamann lifted his hand to touch me, but then he thought better of it. "You don't understand. I have hurt people because of my demon nature. If I hurt you, I could never forgive myself."

"You won't hurt me."

"How do you know?" His eyes burned with anger and sorrow. I had always seen him as the carefree guard who bothered me in the kitchen, but he kept the horrors of his past locked deep in his heart.

"Because I trust you." I refused to let go of him, but I felt him slipping away from me.

"My father is dead because of me." He was trying to push me away to protect me. To protect himself.

"I'm not going anywhere, so stop trying to convince me otherwise."

"Kina." His voice cracked, his pain flowing into his voice and breaking my heart. All I wanted was to make him smile, like he had done for me countless times. "Do you remember how I told you I wasn't afraid of anything?"

"Yes."

"Tonight, I realized that was a lie. When I heard your cry, when I saw that thing ready to kill you, I was terrified of losing you. I'm still terrified of losing you to the point that any distance between us is driving me mad. In this form, my urges are stronger, and I want to take every part of you and mark you as my own, but I'm afraid I won't be able to control myself, and I'll end up hurting you."

I lowered my hands to his chest, desperate to feel his body under my fingers. After nearly dying, I wanted nothing more than to give Reamann every part of me. I needed him to understand that I wasn't afraid of his demon form. I dragged my fingers lower, tracing his V-shaped muscles. "Tonight, I'm yours. Every part of me belongs to you."

A low growl reverberated from his chest. "What if I hurt you?"

"You won't." I craned my neck up, looking into his eyes. I wanted him to see just how much I trusted him.

His chest heaved up and down, struggling to maintain the control he had. "I might lose control in this form." He brought my hand to his mouth before pulling a finger between his lips. He ran his tongue over the digit, and my body shuddered, imagining his tongue elsewhere. It was longer and thicker than I remembered, but I wasn't sure if it was my imagination getting out of control or if his demon form made everything larger.

"I don't care. I want you to lose control. I want you to take me in whatever way you want." I had been treated like a princess my entire life, but it wasn't a life I wanted. I didn't want to be treated like delicate Princess Aukina. I wanted to let loose and know what it was like to live in the raw moment, unfiltered and wild.

Reamann's eyes darkened, his desire threatening to break free. "You might regret that."

"I won't." Out of everything I regretted in my life, being with Reamann was something I knew I'd never regret. "Because I want you. All of you."

The groan that followed from Reamann was nothing short of animalistic. He buried his face in the crook of my neck, his teeth lightly grazing against my throat. Any harder, and he'd rip the flesh open, but I didn't care. My heart raced with fear and excitement, ready to get lost in the demon in front of me.

Chapter 16

Reamann ran his tongue over my skin. My eyes fluttered shut as I took in the sensations, forgetting about the storm raging outside. My head rolled back, exposing my neck to him. If he wanted to, he could rip my throat open, but I knew he would never. He sucked on my neck, lingering over the pulsing veins. "You taste incredible," he muttered against my skin. "I can't wait to taste you everywhere."

He grabbed my ass, making me squeak and squirm, creating friction between my legs. He moved his mouth to my ear. "Shhh, we can't draw attention to ourselves, not with that thing out there." My heart thundered from the brief reminder of the dangers. We should've stopped, but we were both too far gone in our cravings.

He lifted me up, holding me with ease. He was hard beneath me, and I shifted, increasing the friction. I bit my lip to stop myself from moaning, but it was a struggle. I couldn't stop imagining him doing unholy things.

"Reamann," I said breathlessly, growing impatient.

His claws dug into my ass as I pleaded with him, a low growl reverberating in his chest. His need was as strong as mine. He lowered me to the ground before hovering over me. Reamann spread my legs and dove straight into my core. He pushed his tongue inside of me without a warning, and I couldn't hold back the moan that followed. Reamann dug his claws into my thighs as a warning, but it was hard to control my noises with his tongue moving through my folds relentlessly. I shoved my forearm in my mouth to stop the moans that wanted to pour out.

Reamann sucked on my clit, alternating between taking it between his sharp teeth and lapping it with his tongue. The alternating sensations left me reeling. His tongue was better than his fingers ever were. I wanted to cry and scream and plead at the same time. My legs shook from the pleasure surging through my body.

Then he moved lower. He spread my cheeks with his fingers and slid his tongue lower and lower until— I gasped as his tongue swirled around my puckered hole. It was a strange and new sensation, one that felt surprisingly good. When his fingers rubbed against my clit, it pushed my body over its edge. My muscles tightened, and Reamann didn't stop moving his tongue or fingers until my body collapsed with exhaustion.

He wiped his mouth with the back of his hand, taking in my exhausted form. His breath was heavy, and he looked down at me with a hunger that only existed for me. "I didn't want our first time to be like this, but I don't think I can stop now that I've had a taste of you." He kept his hands on my thighs, keeping me spread open for him.

"I need you." My body ached for more. It hungered to be filled with him completely.

He ran his fingers through my folds, taking his time. "There's something you should know." His breathy words were barely audible over the pouring rain. "In this form, I have two dicks."

I knew nothing about demon physiology. I had wondered if his anatomy looked different from a merman's, but I had never imagined two dicks. My mouth watered at the thought of being stuffed full.

I sat up and reached for Reamann's pants, keeping my eyes focused on his. I wanted him in every way possible. I pulled his pants down, and his dicks sprung free. They were stacked on top of one another, and they were thicker than I expected. Ridges ran up the shaft and the tips were reversed heart shaped, coming to a point at the end. I wasn't sure one of them would fit, let alone both of them, but I wasn't the type to back down from a challenge.

I wrapped my fingers around the shaft of the top one and slowly moved my hand back and forth, watching his face closely to make sure I was doing it right.

"Tighter," he ordered, his eyes never leaving mine.

I gripped him harder, but I was afraid to add too much pressure. Male parts were sensitive.

"Tighter." Reamann wrapped his hand around mine and made me squeeze more than I ever would've on my own. He guided my hand up and down his shaft, groaning from the friction. The noises he made burned inside of me. I wanted him to cry out from the pleasure he got directly from me.

"I want you to fuck me," I said.

"With one or two?"

I studied both of his dicks stacked on top of each other. The thought of both of them inside of me was more than I had ever imagined. But to be filled that much. The ache between my legs grew.

"I..." I couldn't decide. I wanted it, but admitting it was difficult.

Reamann grabbed the back of my neck and pulled me into a kiss. He whispered against my mouth. "We'll work our way up to both."

He lifted me up and hovered me over his dicks. I felt one pressing against my entrance while the other one rubbed against my clit. My mouth went dry, eager to feel him inside of me but scared at the same time.

"Hold on, tight," he ordered. I reached for his shoulders, but then he said, "No. Not there."

For a moment, I didn't know where else he might be talking about, but then I focused on his horns. My fingers wrapped around them, and he groaned from the touch alone. I tightened my grip and moved my hands like I did on his cock.

"Fuck, Kina," he muttered, his eyes fluttering half shut. His reaction only pushed me to repeat the motion.

His fingers dug into my hips, and he lowered me onto his cock. My breath hitched, and my hands stopped moving. The only thing I could focus on was the way he filled me up. He lowered me little by little, taking his time, but his face tightened as he struggled to take it slow. He didn't want to hurt me, but I wasn't afraid of that.

When I was sure I could handle him, I whispered, "Fuck me."

His eyes flashed, his animalistic nature threatening to break free. "Kina." He could barely say my name, his control over his body slipping through his fingers.

I moved my hands up and down his horns. "Fuck me," I repeated. I held my chin high, more confident than I had been in a long time. I wanted him.

A growl rumbled from his chest as thunder shook the walls of the building. The sweet, kind Reamann was gone. He lifted me up before slamming me back down. His second dick slid over my clit before pressing into my stomach as his other one moved in and out of my entrance, filling and stretching me in ways I didn't think possible. I gripped his horns until my fingers ached, knowing if I let go, I'd lose my balance.

"You're mine," Reamann grunted, picking up the pace.

"I'm yours," I repeated, knowing I would've said anything to him at that moment. My mind was constantly racing, but with Reamann, I couldn't think about anything other than the way it felt having him deep inside of me. I never wanted it to end, but my body had other plans.

I couldn't control the mewls that rolled off my tongue. Reamann grabbed the back of my head and pressed his mouth against mine, sliding his tongue between my lips to muffle the sounds of my moans. With the friction of both of his dicks, my body was on the verge of falling apart.

Reamann slammed me down one last time and buried his face into the crook of my neck. He bit down, and then his warmth spilled into me. The conflicting sensation pushed me over the edge, and my body pulsed around his cock, wave after wave of pleasure weaving through my muscles.

I barely caught my breath before Reamann picked me up and turned me around.

"What are you doing?" I asked, the exhaustion from two orgasms taking its toll on me.

"I'm only halfway done with you." He set me on my knees and bent me over. He pushed my lower back, making me arch, so my pussy was in the air. He switched which cock he slid into my entrance without a warning. It slid in with ease, since I was soaking from both of our previous highs.

I cried out, pressing my face into the ground. I hadn't expected him to fill me that deeply a second time so quickly. He had only finished with one of his dicks, but the other one was raring to go. Reamann dug his fingers into my hips and plunged into me over and over again, his other cock still hard as it slid over my sensitive bud. Our breaths drowned out the pouring rain, and the rest of the world disappeared. There were no monsters or masters of the house. It was the two of us relishing the way our bodies fit together.

Reamann rubbed his hand over my ass, grabbing and needing the skin. Between my body already being sensitive and his second dick rubbing my clit, it wasn't long before a third orgasm took every last ounce of energy out of me. Reamann finished shortly after, releasing a second load in me.

Before I completely collapsed, he picked me up and pulled me to his chest. I clung to him, never wanting to let him go. There were a thousand worries waiting for us back at the demon king's estate, but at that moment, Reamann was all mine.

Chapter 17

I ran my fingers over Reamann's chest, relishing the coolness of his skin. The rain and thunder continued, and there were no signs of the creature outside. It would've been easy to fall asleep in the demon's arms, but I couldn't close my eyes—not with the thoughts running through my head.

"Reamann?" I whispered, unsure if he was still awake.

He hummed in response. His breathing was steady, but he was awake, staring at the ceiling.

"There's something I need to tell you." After seeing Reamann's vulnerability, it was time for him to learn my secret. Not even Satella knew the truth that slammed against the box I had locked it in the day I left home.

"Are you about to tell me that you're not attracted to demons?" He half-laughed, but it was clear it was a real fear of his.

I lightly smacked his chest. "I think we proved otherwise."

He chuckled as he pulled me on top of his chest. My instinct was to push myself off him, afraid I was going to crush him under my weight, but he grabbed my wrists, refusing to let me go.

"Maybe we should test it out again, just to be sure." His cocks hardened beneath me as if on command.

My mouth watered at the thought, but I refused to let myself get distracted. It was time to stop running. "I didn't tell you the entire truth as to why I ran away from home."

His face hardened as he dropped the jokes. "I'm listening."

I took a labored breath. I didn't want Reamann to look at me any differently once he knew who I was. Seeing his demon form only made me want him more, so I had to believe my other side wouldn't change his opinion of me.

"I was engaged to Prince Sylvar of the Calamity Sea when I left the Hallow Sea. My older sister, Manaia, is the heir to the throne, but as her younger sister, it was my job to solidify relationships with other kingdoms."

My heart roared in my ears. The seconds of silence stretched on.

"So, you're a... princess?" Reamann's face showed no signs of his reaction.

I nodded once. "I had a responsibility to my kingdom, but I swam away. I couldn't take the pressure, and I couldn't imagine marrying someone I didn't love. It felt like I was trapped in a sea cave with no light to guide me out." I closed my eyes, remembering the pain I felt the day I decided to swim far away from everything. It wasn't a decision I made lightly. The thought of never seeing Manaia again was the only thing that nearly made me stay for so long. But when my mother forbade me to step on land again, I couldn't continue on living in the sea.

Reamann sat up, readjusting me on his lap. He wrapped his fingers around my hair, still damp from getting caught in the rainstorm. "Do you want to go home?"

"No." There was no thought behind my response. "The thought of going back to a life that wasn't my own—" I didn't have words to explain, only the racing of my heart. "I miss the sea, but I do not miss that life. I didn't have a choice about who I was or who I wanted to become."

"I can't imagine how difficult it was for you to leave." He dropped my hair and looked away from me. I hated not knowing what was going on behind his ruby eyes.

"Are you mad at me for not telling you sooner?"

"No. I understand why you didn't tell me about your past, and I'd be a hypocrite, since I haven't told you about my own past. We all have our reasons for going to Ethlow."

I hooked my hands around the back of his neck, needing to feel as close to him as possible. Part of me was waiting for everything to fall apart. Sometimes, it felt as if Artagatis cursed me for abandoning my people, and no matter how hard I tried, I only made mistakes.

"Do you ever think about going home?" The moment the words came out of my mouth, I knew it had been the wrong thing to ask.

Reamann's face twisted. "I don't have a home to go back to." My instinct was to ask him why, but the sorrow in his eyes made me hesitate. If he wanted me to know the truth, he'd tell me. "My father died because of me, because of who I am." He gestured to his horns.

I had heard plenty of horror stories about demons, but it was difficult to imagine Reamann hurting his father or anyone else who didn't deserve it. "You don't have to talk about it, if you don't want to."

He shook his head. "No. It's time." He paused, taking a breath, and I waited for him to speak again, afraid to push him too far. "My mother was a demon, but I never knew her, except through the stories my father used to tell. He talked about her as if she was the love of his life, but she left before I was old enough to remember her. My father used to cry when he thought I was asleep. I hated her for leaving me, but I hated her more for making my father cry.

"I tried to be the perfect son for my father. He told me I had to be home before dark every day to keep my true identity a secret. Humans hate demons in the town I was born in, and they'd attack me if they found out the truth—at least that was what he always said. I was late coming home once. I transformed before I made it back to the house, and the villagers saw me. They burned our house down, saying we both deserved to burn in the underworld for deceiving them. I made it out alive, but..."

His voice broke, and the rain filled the silence between us. He didn't need to speak for me to understand what had happened.

I cupped his cheeks, knowing I couldn't take his pain away, but I wanted to try. "That was *not* your fault."

He placed his hand against mine to stop it from shaking. "If I had followed his rules, he'd still be alive."

"You can't think like that. You weren't the one who set the fire. You weren't the one who killed him."

His chest shook as he struggled to calm his emotions. "I can't shake the guilt. I wanted to burn the entire village down, but instead, I ran away. Viridian was the one who found me, broken with nowhere to go. He told me my skills would be useful at Ethlow, so I followed him. I had no other choice. I no longer had a home."

I wrapped my arms around him, wanting to comfort him, but words felt futile. Nothing I said would make the pain of his past go away, but if I proved to him I wasn't going anywhere, maybe it'd heal a small part of him. As I squeezed him, he flinched, making me pull back.

Blood covered my hands, making my throat go dry. "You're hurt," I whispered, my head pounding as I tried to figure out what had happened.

Clicking sounds mixed with the rain, and my body froze. Reamann had dived in front of me to protect me. He had been bleeding since the attack, while we...

The creature moved around the building, searching for us. I held my breath, unable to look away from the blood staining my fingers. The rain had likely washed our scent away, so if we stayed quiet, the creature would leave. At least that was what I hoped.

Reamann put his finger to his mouth, gesturing for me to stay quiet, but I understood the dangers lurking outside. My body shook, remembering how close to death I had gotten from my own stupidity mixed with the creature's attack. Knowing Reamann had risked his life to protect me made my stomach knot.

Reamann extended his claws, ready to fight if the creature found its way inside. He turned his back on me to watch the door, but from that angle, the wounds were clear to me. Two lacerations stretched across his back in an X-shape. They were deep and blood dripped down his bare torso.

Neither of us were breathing as the creature circled around the building. I glanced around the room for anything to help stop the wound from bleeding, but I couldn't see anything from where we were. I didn't dare move, knowing any sound could give away our presence.

I had no idea how long we had been sitting there when clicking sounds finally disappeared. My chest collapsed under the weight of my fear. I moved to the closest crate and tried to pry the lid open, but it only creaked under the pressure.

"What are you doing?" Reamann whispered.

"We have to find something to stop the bleeding." I didn't know if the building would have anything useful, but I couldn't sit still with the gashes in his back leaking blood.

"I'm okay." He followed me to the next crate.

I slammed my hands against the wood, frustration from the night finally coming out. "You're bleeding. We have to stop it before it gets worse. I can't lose you. Not now." My voice cracked. My injured wrist ached, but I didn't care.

Reamann wrapped his arms around me and pulled me against his torso. "You won't lose me. My demon body heals quickly. By morning, I'll be fine."

I refused to turn around. I didn't want him to see my tears when he was the injured one. "You're injured because of me. I can't just sit here and do nothing."

Reamann spun me around and cradled my cheek. "I'm fine. My body will heal on its own. I swear." He pressed his lips against my forehead. It soothed my panic a little, but not enough.

"I will use my shirt to dress the wounds. It'll make me feel better knowing there's something to stop the bleeding." I pulled away to find my damp shirt, and Reamann didn't fight me. He helped me rip my shirt to pieces, so I could tie it around his torso. Satella could've done a better job, but it would suffice until morning.

"You should try to get some rest," Reamann said once I finished dressing his wounds.

My body was exhausted, but the thought of sleeping scared me. "I'm fine."

"Your eyes are drooping. I promise I won't let anything happen to you."

I didn't know how to tell him I was worried about him, not me. "As long as you're awake, I'm awake."

He smiled, but it didn't quite reach his eyes. "Come here." He pulled me into his lap and guided my head to his chest. I listened to his heartbeat, a reminder that he was okay, that he was alive. I focused on the rhythm of his heart, and it wasn't long before my body betrayed me.

The birds chirping outside sounded louder than I was used to. I cracked my eyes open, and my entire body ached. I didn't want to move, but the ground was hard and uncomfortable. I pushed myself up, slowly orienting myself and remembering everything that happened. Ovid. The attack. Reamann.

My body was peppered with bruises, and I was sure only some of them could be blamed on the creature. The ones on my thighs were from a very different activity. The spot between my shoulder and neck was particularly sore, and when my fingers brushed over it, scabs scraped against my fingers in the shape of a bite mark. I was dressed in an unfamiliar shirt, but I didn't remember how I got into it.

The door to the building creaked, making me jump, but when Reamann walked through the doors, I relaxed. His skin was back to its regular tone, and his body had shrunk—not that he was small in his human form. He froze, a frown forming on his lips as he took me in.

"It's safe to head back to the estate," he said.

The light outside was soft. The sun had barely crested over the horizon, but the night was over, which meant the monsters of the shadows had crawled back into the depths they belonged in.

"Were you up all night?" I wasn't ready to return to my other life just yet, knowing there was at least one lecture waiting for me, if not worse.

Reamann nodded. "The rain washed away our scent, so nothing else bothered us." He didn't move closer, and my stomach twisted. After last night, all I wanted was to touch him again, but he didn't seem to feel the same.

Before I could get in my head, I crossed the room, not stopping until I was directly in front of him. "What's wrong?"

His eyes immediately went to my neck. "I hurt you."

I felt him retreating, his fears coming to life, but I needed him to understand that wasn't how I felt. I grabbed his hand and pressed it over my heart. "Last night was incredible, and I wouldn't change anything about it. Well, except the giant creature trying to kill both of us."

I waited for his laughter, but it didn't come. I wasn't going to let the memory of last night get tainted now that our urges weren't driving our desires. I lifted onto my toes and grabbed the back of his neck, pulling him down until our lips were a breath away. "I regret nothing that happened last night, so don't you dare regret it either, because I have plans for those two dicks."

Reamann's entire body relaxed, and then he closed the distance between us. I only pulled away once I was sure his worries had faded, even if it was only a little. "We should get back to the estate. I'm sure others will be worried we've been gone all night."

Worried was an understatement. The moment we walked through the doors of the estate, Nyri threw her hands around me. "Thank the goddesses you're still alive! I wanted to search for you, but Zathrian wouldn't let me." The demon king stood a few feet behind Nyri, looking guilty.

"I couldn't leave and risk the others, and I wasn't about to let Nyri go anywhere without me." Zathrian pressed his lips into a thin line. After years of him being an invisible presence, he wasn't anything like I had imagined. He was softer, but there was a real chance that was Nyri's doing. He was wrapped around her finger.

"It's okay. Reamann kept me safe." I tightened my grip on his hand, wishing everyone hadn't been there the moment we walked through the door. I was exhausted and wanted to clean up before others saw the blood crusted on my neck.

"He shouldn't have had to protect you, leaving his post the entire night." Viridian stood behind everyone else, but his presence was daunting, especially with the little shadows dancing off his shoulders.

The demon king lifted his hand. "I think these two have been through enough. They don't need to be scolded."

Viridian bristled, but he didn't argue. "Yes, sire." My stomach twisted into a knot, sensing this wasn't the end of Viridian's criticisms.

I turned to Nyri, the guilt from yesterday returning. "I'm sorry I couldn't stop him from stealing the flower and causing everyone to worry. I thought..." The words caught in my throat. I had wanted to make a difference by stopping Ovid, because it felt like he stole the flower because of me.

Nyri took my hands. "I'm just glad you're okay. The flower doesn't matter as much as you." She smiled, and it was genuine. I had expected her to be more upset, but the demon king and Viridian looked more perturbed than her. "Now, you and Reamann go see Satella. She'll be thrilled to know you're both okay. She was probably more worried than me."

Neither of us argued, knowing we had caused enough worry for a lifetime.

Chapter 18

Wistari barely said anything to me all day, which was unlike the talkative elf. Usually, she prattled on about who was mad at who and all the other ongoings at the estate. Her silence unnerved me, but I didn't know if I should ask her if everything was okay or not, so I kept quiet.

Only when she had set a dish on the counter a little too hard, did I approach her. The dinner rush had faded, giving us a moment of privacy.

"Okay, what's going on with you?" It wasn't like the girl to throw a fit.

Wistari pursed her lips, glaring at me. "What's up with me?" Her tone made me hunker down, realizing her anger was directed at me. "You ran off in a storm at dusk to try to stop a man who has hurt you before, like some hero. But you're not. You're not a hero, and you did a stupid thing that almost got you killed. If Reamann hadn't been able to find you..." She squeezed her eyes shut and tightened her hands into little fists. "You could've died out there, and you would've been the only one to blame."

I had no words to defend myself. I had known leaving the estate was a risk, but I hadn't thought I could help. I wanted to do good, but I only caused issues. There was only one thing I could say. "I'm sorry. I didn't mean to worry you."

Wistari let a long breath out from her nose before opening her eyes. "Well, you did. I couldn't sleep not knowing you were okay, and then you come back like nothing happened, even though you're covered in bruises. You need to stop worrying about everyone else and worry about yourself for once. Take a day off. Rest, heal, find a hobby. Do something other than waste your life away in this kitchen."

I swallowed hard, no words coming to mind. I wasn't about to tell her the truth behind those bruises—she was too young to hear something like that.

But she was right.

All I ever did was spend my life in the kitchen. I told myself it was because I loved cooking, which was true to an extent. I liked making others happy with my cooking, and I liked being in control. It was why I stepped up and spent nearly all of my free time cooking, even though Cibil was the head of the kitchen. It had all been fine. I had been building a life for myself, one that wasn't assigned to me at birth.

But I didn't want to continue on like that. I wanted to build a life with Reamann, but that would never happen if I spent most of my time in the kitchen. It was time I took a step back and asked Viridian to assign someone else to the kitchen for extra help. I didn't know if it was possible. In order to get help, we would either have to get a new resident at Ethlow—which didn't happen often—or he'd have to delegate help from other areas. Before, I hadn't wanted to take attention from other assignments because it was selfish.

Maybe it was time to be a little selfish.

"I'll be better," I said, straightening my spine. I hated the thought of Wistari being upset with me.

"I don't want you to be better. I want you to be happy and alive." Wistari took a step back. "I'm going to call it for the night. You should, too."

I didn't stop the elf from leaving. We were the last ones in the kitchen after a long day. There was more to do. The kitchen was a mess, and nothing was prepared for breakfast. My body itched to move to finish things up. I was exhausted after a long night of sleeping on the floor, but silence slinked through the air, a harsh reminder of everything I had messed up.

I needed to rest, but there was too much to do. I had to work hard to prove I was worthy, that I hadn't wasted my life by running away from my royal responsibilities. I had to show everyone that I could do something right.

But I was exhausted. I couldn't find the energy to work, so I stood still, unable to decide what to do.

"I thought I'd find you here." Reamann's voice broke through the silence. He sounded happy to see me, and I knew the moment I turned around, his dazzling smile would melt my heart. He wanted me, despite everything that happened. He didn't see me as the broken mermaid I was. "Kina?" he called out softly, worry lacing his voice.

I turned, unable to stop the tears from bubbling in my eyes. I wanted to be strong and act like I was fine after last night, but I was anything but.

The half-demon's eyes widened, and he rushed over to me. "What's wrong?"

"We almost died last night, and it's all my fault." The reality crashed down like a tree struck by lightning. Wistari's words sank in, stripping away any sense of courage I had been trying to hold on to. "It feels like everything's my fault, and I don't know what to do. I feel like one wrong step will send me crashing into the abyss. I can't seem to do anything right."

Reamann's strong arm wrapped around my waist, and his hand held my head against his chest. He made me feel safe, which made my walls crumble to the floor. My tears turned to sobs, and I couldn't stop. It was as if I had been holding a mask to hide the cracks in my life for years, but I didn't have the strength to hold it anymore.

When I didn't stop crying, Reamann picked me up and carried me to my room. He locked the door behind us and set me on my bed. It was a small mattress, not meant for two people, especially with one my size, but that didn't stop him from sliding into the bed and pulling me to his chest, letting me cry in his arms until I fell asleep.

The next morning I didn't get up until after breakfast.

For the next week, I let Wistari and the others handle the mornings, letting myself sleep in properly for the first time at Ethlow. I went to the kitchen with plenty of time before lunch, which was a strange feeling, but my body felt lighter. I hadn't realized how lack of sleep had made me feel drained on a daily basis. I pushed through that physical exhaustion to prove to everyone I could handle the kitchen, but I didn't want to do that any longer.

As the crowd thinned after dinner, Reamann walked into the mess hall, and my entire face lit up. I dropped what I was doing and rushed over, throwing myself at him. He picked me up, spinning me around before kissing me deeply, not caring who saw us.

"I can't decide if you two are cute or disgusting," Wistari called out from the kitchen. Ever since I started taking the mornings off, her mood had lightened, and she acted as if everything was okay between us, which I was grateful for.

"You'll understand when you're in love one day," Reamann called out.

My grip tightened on him. "Love?" I repeated. We hadn't said that to each other, but we had spent as much time together as we could with our different schedules.

Reamann's mouth gaped open as a realization dawned on him. Then he smiled, brushing the back of his hand against my cheek. "I love you, Kina."

I grabbed the back of his head and pulled him into a kiss. I never thought someone would say those words to me, especially not someone like Reamann, someone kind and caring.

"Follow me," I said, an idea filling my head. I grabbed his hand and pulled him into the kitchen. There were lingering residents getting their dinners after the crowd, but I was sure the others could handle the kitchen for a few moments. "We'll be right back," I told Wistari. "We're going to just check on supplies."

"We are?" Reamann asked, and I tugged on his arm, ignoring his comment.

I led him to the supplies closet, shutting the door behind us. There wasn't a lock on the door, but I didn't care. I pushed Reamann against the door and grabbed his shirt, pulling him into a kiss.

"Is this your definition of checking on supplies?" Reamann murmured against my lips.

"Uh-huh." I tightened my fingers around his neck, distracting him with my tongue. I didn't want to think about others or our dwindling time together. Soon it'd be dark, and he'd have to leave for his guard shift. He couldn't afford to be late with Viridian breathing down both of our necks.

Reamann inhaled sharply, struggling to control his urges. His hardness pressed against me, showing just how much he wanted this. "The others could hear us."

"Want me to stop?" I looked up at him with wide eyes, trying to look as innocent as possible.

"Don't you dare." He slid his fingers into my hair and pulled our mouths together. He slipped his tongue into my mouth, and I parted my lips, needing to taste him.

My hand moved over his muscular torso, barely hidden by the armor dressing his body. His chest rumbled beneath my touch. We both barely kept our clothes on but the thought of the young elf hearing us stopped me from reaching into his pants.

When we broke apart, our breaths filled the air. Our desires hung between us. We had barely been able to control ourselves since the attack.

Reamann held me close, nuzzling my hair and running his hands over my body. "You do things to me that no one has ever done before."

"Oh?"

"It's like I can't get enough of you. You are an addiction, and I don't want to stop."

I bit my lip as happiness filled my chest. Between taking more time to myself and falling deeper in love with Reamann, my life was finally coming together. "Good, because I don't want you to ever stop."

Reamann groaned, as if struggling with his own desires. "If I wasn't worried about Wistari walking in on us, this would only be the beginning of a long evening."

"Shame. I had some dirty things planned for us." I pulled away and reached for the door, but Reamann was already on me.

"Just a moment longer," he whispered into my neck. "I want you to myself for a little longer."

I didn't fight him, melting into his arms instead. "I've been thinking about something recently that I need your help with."

"Oh?" He kissed my neck, making it difficult to focus.

"What do you think about starting a training class for people who want to learn to defend themselves? After everything with Ovid and that creature, it made me wish I knew how to fight. I don't want to feel helpless, and I thought others might feel the same."

Reamann hummed against my skin. "That's a great idea."

"Will you help me with it?" I asked, excitement bubbling in my chest for two reasons.

He ran his tongue up my neck before sucking on the sensitive spot behind my ear. "Only if you promise to be there every step of the way."

"I think I can do that." I bit my lower lip to contain a moan. "Come on. We should go before others get suspicious." I pulled free from Reamann's grip, but it didn't stop him from trying to capture me again.

We tumbled through the storage room, laughing and nearly losing our balance, but I quickly realized we weren't alone.

"Master Viridian." I barely found my footing, quickly losing my smile. The demon was a jump scare.

"Miss Aukina, there is a visitor here for you." Viridian's eyes flashed, distaste forming the shape of his mouth. He knew exactly what we had been doing. There were no secrets from the master of the house.

"A visitor?" It didn't make sense. There were no visitors at Ethlow.

"Yes," Viridian confirmed. He likely already saw the confusion running through my thoughts. "Your mother is here to see you."

Chapter 19

T he world spun round and round and round. I couldn't remember how to breathe properly. Viridian was messing with me. It was the only explanation for the words that had just left his mouth.

"You must be mistaken." My voice croaked as I struggled to restrain the fear surging through my veins.

Reamann pressed his hand against my lower back for support, but he couldn't understand what this meant.

"I am never mistaken. She is waiting for you at the front and expects your presence with haste." Viridian's eyes burned into me, annoyed by my hesitation. He expected everything to happen in a timely manner.

Just like my mother. She expected everything on her timeline with no regard for others. It had been nearly six years since I last saw her, yet I was confident she hadn't changed.

"You don't have to see her if you don't want to," Reamann said. He was sweet but naive.

"I would advise against that," Viridian said. After only a few moments with my mother, the master of the house knew better than to go against her wishes.

I squeezed Reamann's hand. "No, it's fine. The longer I keep her waiting, the worse it will be." My words weren't a comfort to him, but they weren't meant to be.

"I'm coming with you." Reamann held my hand as if he was afraid to let go. I hadn't told him much about my previous life, but he knew enough to understand this wasn't going to be an easy conversation.

Viridian's eyes flicked between Reamann and me before he let out an exaggerated breath through his nose. "Follow me."

We moved through the estate, making our way to the grand entrance. I didn't say anything, trying to prepare myself for my mother. There was only one reason she'd come to Ethlow: to bring me home. She couldn't force me. She'd try to use guilt, but now that I had Reamann, I couldn't stand the thought of leaving Ethlow to go back to my old life.

My mother stood in the entrance with four bodyguards flanking her. She was a large woman with long black hair and brown eyes that matched my own. She was taller than me, and the way she stood made her seem like the largest figure in the room. She wore gold and green—the colors of our kingdom. The guards next to her were mostly women, and they shifted and tugged at their clothing. Most merfolk didn't venture onto land often if ever, unlike me. In the sea, we didn't need clothes.

Before she noticed me, I pulled my hand away from Reamann out of instinct. She had no say over my life, but I didn't want her to comment on a boyfriend—not when the last time I saw her I was engaged to be married.

"Queen Fetia, I have brought your daughter as requested."
Viridian bowed his head, showing more respect to my mother than
he showed most of the residents. The only other being I had seen
him bow his head to was the demon king, but if he knew I was a
princess, would that change?

Queen Fetia's attention narrowed on me in an instant. I stood
tall and held my chin high, just like the princess I was raised to
be. She stepped closer, her guards following her every movement.
They held tridents at their sides, ready to protect their queen in
case of an attack. Hallow Sea warriors were highly skilled in the
water, but on land, I had a feeling they'd be no match for someone
like Viridian.

"You've lost weight," Queen Fetia said. "Are they not feeding
you enough here?"

I ran my fingers over my plush stomach. I was one of the rounder
residents in Ethlow, so it was strange to hear someone comment on
my weight loss. "Everything I need is provided for me here."

She huffed before turning her attention to Reamann, making
both of us tense. "I see you've been assigned a personal guard.
At least the demon king has some sort of sense. Although, he
should've sent you home the moment you showed up on his
doorstep."

Viridian smiled, flashing his mouth full of sharp teeth—something he rarely did. "I suggest you choose your words wisely,
Queen Fetia. As royalty, you are a welcomed guest, but that can
change if you do not show my king the respect he deserves."

Queen Fetia smiled back, showing her own mouth full of sharp teeth. "Looks like you've got a little bite to you. Do not fret. My business here is with my daughter, and that will be over quickly."

"If you've come to ask me to come home, then you have wasted your time," I said. My mouth was dry, and my body itched for freedom. I wanted to break free of my human skin and swim far, far away from my mother, but there was no swimming from this. Not any longer.

"I wish to speak to my daughter in private," she said, shooting glares in Viridian's and Reamann's direction. "This is a personal matter, one I do not wish to share with demons."

"Yes, madam." Viridian bowed, but his eyes flashed with irritation. He likely wasn't going far. He stepped back, disappearing into the shadows.

When Reamann didn't move, my mother flared her nostrils. "Are you dull? I said leave. My daughter does not need your services any longer."

Before Reamann could respond, I grabbed his hand. "Reamann is not going anywhere, and he is not my bodyguard. He is my boyfriend, and he stays."

Queen Fetia puffed her chest. "By boyfriend, I pray to Artagatis that you do not mean you let this boy defile you."

Reamann tightened his grip on my hand, and the tension in the air grew palpable.

The best response was to ignore her comment. No matter what I had said, it wouldn't change the past. "Why are you here, Queen Fetia?"

"Queen Fetia?" she repeated. "Do you not acknowledge me as your mother anymore? Has this place changed you to be so cruel?"

"You've never treated me like a daughter, just a tool to grow your kingdom." I loved my father and my sister, but my mother and I had always had a tense relationship.

"You left without saying goodbye, like an ungrateful child. Do you know what kind of damage you did to our relations with the Calamity Sea? How do you think the prince reacted when we had to tell him his promised bride disappeared to live on land? It's worse than you imagined." The venom in her voice made me flinch. Part of me wanted to recoil and run, but with Reamann watching, I couldn't let myself shrink.

"Why are you here?" I repeated. I wasn't interested in reliving the past.

"I am here to take you home." There was no room to argue with her tone—there never had been.

"I am not going home." I held my chin high, pretending to be the royalty I had been groomed to be. I wouldn't let her intimidate me into a life I couldn't stand.

"Manaia, the once future queen, is dead, which means you are the only remaining heir to the Hallow Sea throne." Queen Fetia's face hardened, baring the same ice her heart was made out of. "I have let you run wild for long enough, and I am putting a stop to this little tantrum."

It felt like I was punched in the gut. My sister was dead, and I didn't know what to say. It didn't feel real. I hadn't seen her in years. In my head, she was in the Hallow Sea, preparing to be queen. She wasn't dead.

"I... I can't." I wasn't queen material. I could barely handle the princess life. "Let Sefina take over."

"Your cousin is not fit to rule."

"And I am?" My heart thumped like drums, signaling the end of my life. It grew louder and louder, making it nearly impossible to stand still.

"You will need training, but you have time before you have to take over, so we can shape you into whom the kingdom needs."

The drums slammed against my skull. "I can't."

Queen Fetia grabbed my wrist. "You abandoned your family once. I will not let you do it again."

Reamann grabbed the queen's arm. "Let go of her."

The queen's guards pointed their tritons at Reamann, and the world around me cracked. It was too much.

Queen Fetia sneered at Reamann. "I will bring my daughter home, even if it means bringing war on this place. I'm sure the demon king would not want others to know he's been keeping the future queen of the Hallow Sea as a captive."

"You can't just take Kina," Reamann growled.

The world spun, and I felt like I was going to be sick. "Stop it," I whispered.

"I gave birth to Aukina. I will be taking her one way or another. How is up to her."

Reamann was ready to fight my mother, and her guards were ready to attack him. It was all too much.

I pulled my arm free and stumbled back. "I have to go." I didn't know where I was going, but I turned and ran, not stopping until I couldn't breathe.

Chapter
20

T he library was strangely quiet. The kitchen and the mess
hall were always buzzing with cacophony, which had been
a welcomed distraction, but not today. I wanted the silence to
consume me. The library felt like the only place to let that happen.
No one would look for me here.

I walked through the stacks and stacks of books, wondering
what it was like to enjoy reading. Learning to read and write in
common had been nothing but a struggle, so the thought of reading for fun had never occurred to me. With the emptiness in the
room, it didn't seem to occur to many.

I picked up a book with black edges. A layer of dust covered the
top of the book, and the title was written in golden swirls against
the dark cover. I didn't recognize the language of the title.

"What are you doing here?"

I squeaked and dropped the book.

Tareen pushed past me and grabbed the book, brushing it off.
She was the estate's librarian, but I didn't see her often. She was one
of the residents that grabbed lunch and ran off elsewhere to eat.
She was always dressed in black, and her brown curls hung wildly
around her head.

"Sorry," I said, my shoulders sinking. So much for silence.

"You don't read, so why are you here?" Tareen's tone bordered on accusatory, and I wasn't sure how to respond. She didn't look upset, especially as she stared at me with her doll-like eyes and freckles. She seemed harmless.

"I wanted somewhere I could think. Is that okay?" I didn't know where else I'd go if she said no.

She pushed the book back onto the shelf. "Just don't throw any more books on the ground, and I suppose you can stay."

"I will keep my hands to myself like a sinking sea slug."

Tareen furrowed her brows. "I don't know what that is. You're a little weird." The librarian walked away, but I found myself following her.

"What do you mean by that?"

Tareen weaved in and out of the bookcases, as if she didn't care if the conversation continued. "I didn't mean that offensively. People think I'm a little weird, too. I'm pretty sure most people don't like me."

The librarian's statement made me ache for her. I always assumed she liked eating alone, which was why she avoided the mess hall and stayed in the library by herself most of the time. "Maybe people don't know you."

"Maybe." She stopped suddenly, and I nearly ran into her. "Is there a reason why you're following me?"

Her question threw me off, and I didn't know how to answer, since I didn't know why I was following her. "I just thought we could talk."

She tilted her head to the side, making her curls bounce. "I thought you came here to be alone."

She was right, but the silence scared me more than I wanted to admit. "I don't know."

Tareen glanced behind her, and I prepared for her to leave. "Do you like tea? I don't, but I know that's something people drink when they're upset, and I don't really have anything else to offer you. Unless you want juice. I could get fruit from the kitchen, or—"

"It's okay." I placed my hand on her arm and offered a smile. "Tea sounds fine."

Tareen pulled back, cringing at my touch. "Great. Right this way." She led me down a series of bookcases until she found a wall that was open. She knocked twice, causing a section in the wall to disappear. "This is my private quarters, so don't go telling everyone about it."

"I'm as tight-lipped as a rainbow clam."

The door led to a dark hallway. Tareen waved her hand, creating a ball of light that followed above her head. The passage was longer than I had anticipated, but it led to a wide room. There were bottles on nearly every surface and a strong scent of sage in the air. A soft meow came from the depths of the room, but I didn't see the creature the noise belonged to.

"That's Binx. He's shy around other people, so you won't see him." Tareen moved to a large cauldron and snapped her fingers, lighting a fire in an instant. As she waited for the water to boil, she found a stone cup and threw in loose leaves in it. Then she added the hot water and handed it to me.

The scent was strong, making me recoil a little. I muttered a thank you, unsure if accepting the witch's offer was smart.

"If you finish the drink, I can read your tea leaves. Maybe that will help with whatever is perplexing you," Tareen said. She scurried around, casually kicking objects to the side in an attempt to declutter.

"I didn't say anything about having a problem."

Tareen made a face. "You didn't have to. You're not subtle with your thoughts. Let me guess. Boy trouble? I heard you were dating that fire head demon."

I sipped the tea to give me time to contemplate my next words. I didn't want to talk about my problem with Satella and Nyri. I didn't want to admit to them that I was considering going home, since I was sure they'd protest. But I wasn't close to Tareen. She didn't care if I stayed or went, which meant she'd have a neutral opinion.

"My mother came to Ethlow to bring me back home, so I can take my dead sister's place as future queen of the Hallow Sea." The words didn't feel real. I wanted to believe that this was some elaborate ruse that Queen Fetia created to get me to go home, and Manaia would be waiting for me back in the Hallow Sea. But my mother wasn't that cruel. She'd never lie about her daughter dying. It would only lead to bad karma from Artagatis.

Tareen's eyes widened, and she returned to attempting to clean. "So you've been a secret princess all this time?"

"Yeah." I cringed after another long sip of tea. It tasted horrible.

"And you chose this life?" Tareen asked.

I felt myself shrinking. "Here, I'm free. There, everything is decided for me."

Tareen was quiet for a long moment. "What happens if you don't go home?"

"My mother says she'll start a war on the demon king, but I don't think she'll go that far. She is all talk."

Tareen crinkled her nose. "Are you sure about that? If war comes to the estate, it'll put a lot of innocents in danger."

My chest tightened. When the witch put it that way, it didn't feel like I had a choice, but the thought of leaving tore me apart. "I have a cousin that can take over as queen. I can make my mother see reason." Sefina was young. She was only ten when I left, but she had time to grow into a strong ruler.

"It doesn't sound like she's the reasonable type, if she's threatening war to get you to go home." Tareen looked at me with wild eyes, slamming guilt into my chest.

I didn't want to go back to the life of a princess with everything planned for me. I didn't want to become queen. I didn't want to leave Reamann. He had become a beacon of life, and I had never been happier.

"The life of a ruler is one of many sacrifices." Tareen plucked my empty cup from my hand and inspected the tea leaves at the bottom. She wrinkled her nose. "You have a difficult choice ahead of you, but with the heart of a queen, you'll make the right choice."

The heart of a queen.

That felt like a joke. I had the heart of a coward, not a queen.

Chapter
21

I checked the barracks in search of Reamann, but he wasn't there. I had to see him one last time before embarking on a life I didn't want. Crows circled the estate as I made my way back to the building, and they felt like a dark omen. Last time one appeared, I nearly died. This time, a part of me would die with the decision I made.

My feet slowed, knowing each step brought me closer to a decision I didn't want to make. I thought about Manaia. We were never close like other sisters, but she had been there when I needed her most. The thought of never seeing her again cut a hole in my heart. Taking her place as queen filled that hole with despair.

I searched the estate, looking everywhere I thought my mother wouldn't be. After seeing that the kitchen was empty, I went to my room. Reamann sat on my bed, staring at his hands.

"I've been looking for you." I shut the door behind me. The last remnants of light flickered out, and as darkness took over, Reamann shifted into demon form. The bed dipped under him as he grew larger, his skin cracking and darkening. His eyes glowed in the dimness of the room.

"You're leaving, aren't you?" he whispered.

Every part of me wanted to rush over to him and throw myself at him. He was everything I ever wanted and everything I could never have. "I don't have a choice."

Reamann jumped to his feet. "You always have a choice, Kina. You can choose to stay. Don't go back to a life you don't want."

"My sister is dead, and if I don't go, my mother will attack the estate." My voice cracked, the statement feeling closer to reality. "If others die because of me, I'll never forgive myself."

"We'll fight for you. We'll do whatever it takes to stop her from taking you."

"It's not that simple. My sister died when I wasn't there, and someone has to take her place. I can't just walk away from her memory."

"You have to stop living for everyone else. Live for yourself for once." His voice was harsh and unlike him.

"I am Princess Aukina of the Hallow Seas. I do not have the luxury of living for myself." I held my chin high, trying to suppress my emotions, like I was taught to do.

Reamann removed the space between us and grabbed my arms. In his demon form, I had to strain my neck to look up into his beautiful red eyes. "Please, don't go. I can't lose you." The way his voice cracked nearly undid me.

"I have to go, but I know you'll be okay." I cupped his cheek, wanting the moment to last forever.

"Not without you." Tears rolled down his eyes. "I'll follow you if that's what it takes."

"Reamann—" The last bit of my composure broke seeing his tears. "Where I'm going, you can't follow. If I could stay—"

"You can. Zathrian won't let your mother take you against your will. Nyri won't allow it. I won't allow it. Just stay, and we'll figure it out. Please." Before I could argue, he grabbed the back of my head and pulled me into a deep kiss. I tasted his pain and desperation, and I wanted to take away all of his hurt. But how could I when I was the cause of it?

I ran my hands over his chest, feeling his muscular body that was bursting out of his clothes. He pulled me closer, leaving no space between us. I clawed at his chest, desperate to feel his skin. The thought of leaving tore me to pieces, but as I dove deeper into the moment with Reamann, it healed the cracks that threatened to tear me apart completely.

Our clothes disappeared piece by piece, and when nothing else separated us, Reamann picked me up. I wrapped my legs around his waist, and felt him pressed against my core. My mouth watered as I thought about both of his dicks. He carried me to the bed and set me down. His eyes glowed with pain. The only thing I could do was prolong the full breadth of his anguish.

I reached between us, wrapping my fingers around one of his dicks. He groaned, flashing his sharp teeth. A surge of energy and determination burst through me, urging me to keep going. If I couldn't give Reamann the rest of my life, I wanted to give him every other part of me.

"I need you," I whispered. "All of you."

"Are you sure?" he asked, but his eyes burned bright with desire.

"Yes."

Reamann kissed me, but he didn't linger. He kissed down my jaw and neck. He sucked and nipped along my collarbones, leaving marks that would linger for days after. He took his time kissing my stomach. I sucked in my gut as a habit, as if holding my breath would hide the weight on my body, but Reamann didn't care. He kissed my curves as if he enjoyed every part of me.

He moved lower, spreading my legs. He licked his lips as he looked at my core, enjoying the sight. My heart raced with anticipation, and when he dove head first into my pussy, my body jerked from the pleasure. He ran his tongue through my folds, and I fisted my bed sheets, unable to think about anything except the way his tongue moved in and out of me.

A familiar pressure built in my core, but Reamann lowered himself, spreading my cheeks. His tongue explored my crack, and this time I was better prepared for the sensation. His tongue swirled around my puckered hole, and when he pushed inside, I gasped, surprised by how good it felt. He worked my opening, slowly stretching and preparing me for more. At the same time, he pushed his finger into my pussy, working both of my openings. The combined sensations sent my body into overdrive, and it wasn't long before waves of pleasure crashed over me.

As my body came down from its high, Reamann readjusted. He slid both of his dicks through my arousal, coating himself thoroughly. He lined himself up at both of my entrances before leaning forward to kiss me. "I love you," he whispered.

I wanted to tell him I loved him back, but the words wouldn't come out. This was the last night I'd spend with Reamann, and telling him I loved him right before leaving felt like a punishment. I didn't deserve his love. I didn't deserve to share that moment with him, but I couldn't stop myself from pulling him into a kiss to distract myself from what my life was about to become.

I dug my fingers into his neck. "Fuck me," I pleaded, needing more than his lips to distract me.

Reamann groaned and pushed himself forward, stretching out both of my holes. He moved slowly, wanting to be careful, but I didn't want that.

"Don't stop." I wanted him to see how much I needed him. I didn't want him to hold back. I wanted him to give into his carnal desires.

He pushed deeper, but it wasn't enough. I bit his lip, wanting to fuel his demon desires. He growled and pushed all the way into me. I had never felt so full in my life, and I loved every second of it. I felt nothing like a princess with a demon inside of me, filling me completely with both of his dicks.

"Fuck me," I said when he didn't move right away.

He rolled his hips, creating friction as he moved in and out of me. "Fuck, Kina. You feel so good."

I loved knowing that I was making Reamann feel good with my body alone. "Harder." He responded to my command, moving faster and harder. The sound of our skin slapping together mixed with our mewls. When the sensations became too much for my body to handle, I dug my nails into Reamann's back, leaving scratches behind.

"Reamann," I muttered, but he captured my mouth before I could finish. He already knew I was close, because he knew me and my body.

Pleasure like I had never felt before exploded through my muscles. My walls pulsed around Reamann's cock, which was enough to push him over the edge. He slammed into me one last time before spilling his seed. We stayed like that, only the sound of our breaths filling the air.

Reamann was the first one to pull away. He went to the bathroom connected to my room and brought back a damp towel. He carefully cleaned me up before slipping back into the bed and pulling me onto his chest. I rested my head against his pecs and listened to his heartbeat, neither of us saying anything. Any other day, I would've fallen asleep listening to the steady thrum of his heart, but not tonight.

I couldn't sleep, knowing my time was running out.

The moon peered through the window, watching as I pulled on boots meant for a long journey. Reamann was fast asleep on my bed, and I resisted the urge to lean in and kiss him, afraid to disturb his slumber. If he asked me to stay, I would have, despite the dangers it could bring. My guard had completely fallen, which was why I had to leave before he woke.

Queen Fetia sat in the Grand Hall, as if she knew I would show up. She appeared to be alone, but her guards hid in the shadows, watching my every move. She held a book as if she was reading.

"How did you find me?" I asked, taking a seat next to her. Ethlow was deep on land, and no one knew my identity at the estate.

"You shifted into your mermaid form, and I followed that pulse. You didn't think you could hide from me forever, did you?" She flipped the page, but her eyes didn't follow the words.

"Is Manaia really dead?" She wouldn't tell me the truth if she had been lying from the beginning, but I needed to hear her say it again before I threw everything I worked for away.

"She snuck away from the palace without guards. She couldn't defend herself against the sudden attack. She wanted to be more like you." She spoke as if they were simple facts, not the way her own daughter died.

"Like me?"

"She admired your free spirit. Despite your betrayal to our family, she talked about you as if you were some hero. She wanted to honor you. It's time you come home to honor her."

I took a long moment to speak. Manaia was dead. It didn't feel real, but that'd change once I got back to the sea, and she wasn't there. "Will you really rage war if I don't go with you?"

"What do you think?" It was a loaded question, not an answer. How far would a queen go to bring her only remaining heir home?

"I will go."

"I'm surprised I'm not going to have to drag you out of here kicking and screaming," Queen Fetia said. She wrinkled her nose. "We will make sure to wash the scent of that demon off you before returning home. We won't have your propriety to bargain for your hand in marriage, but you'll be queen. Plenty will accept that."

I placed a brick around my heart, knowing this was the beginning of building up a wall around my emotions. "His name is Reamann, and he is more than just a demon. And I didn't have my propriety before leaving the Hallow Sea."

My mother snapped the book shut. "I don't care who he is, as long as you are leaving him behind." She ignored my last statement. She had a habit of omitting things she didn't want to hear.

I wanted to scream at her for her terrible words. The thought of leaving Reamann behind was almost enough to change my mind. "I will only go back to the Hallow Sea on one condition. I will not take a husband. I will reign as queen as the sole ruler."

My mother's flicker of shock shifted to irritation. I had never stood up to her before. "Do you think you have the power to negotiate?"

No.

But I had to try.

"If I choose to stay, there are warriors who will fight to protect me. You will have to spend kingdom resources on a fight you will likely lose. Either you accept my condition, or I will not go willingly."

Something like pride flickered in her eyes. "Fine. As long as you understand that you will have to produce an heir, whether or not you marry."

"Fine." A compromise was better than I could've expected. "We have to leave at dawn. No later."

My mother stood, smiling triumphantly. She never had a doubt that she'd be able to bring me home with her. My stomach churned, unable to shake the feeling of being manipulated. "We leave now."

I looked at the windows that were blocked by thick curtains, keeping out the darkness of the night. "It's too dangerous to leave at night."

"Don't worry. I've made arrangements with King Zathrian. He understands the urgency to leave right away, and he has assured safe passage out of this demon-ridden land." She snapped her fingers, but nothing happened.

A few moments later, the shadows burst from the corner of the room, and Viridian stepped into the open. "I am not a servant for you to call on at your will."

Queen Fetia's smile made the master of the house bristle. "I was promised that you will be my personal escort out of this place. Is that not true?"

Viridian smiled, but his eyes were dark with the desire to kill. He stretched his fingers, flashing his sharp nails, but then he returned to his usual composure. I couldn't imagine talking to the demon that way, but Queen Fetia wasn't afraid. She acted like a true queen—something I wasn't sure I could ever manage.

"Yes, madam," Viridian said. "As long as those leaving with you are willing." He only looked at the queen. If he glanced in my direction, he would've seen my moment of doubt.

"Yes. Don't waste any more of my time." She walked towards the door, her guards emerging from the shadows to walk with her, none of them bothering to glance back at me even once.

Viridian hesitated, turning to me. "I have to say, I'm shocked by your decision."

I swallowed, surprised by the demon's comment. I had expected Viridian to be the first one to usher me away from Ethlow with the headaches I had caused him of late. "I have responsibilities."

"Yes." He looked me up and down. "I have worked at Ethlow for longer than you can imagine, and one thing I have learned is that those who end up at Ethlow do not belong out there."

I opened my mouth, offended by his comment. It felt as if he was saying I couldn't make it out there on my own, but there was no use in arguing with him. I picked up my skirt, knowing I couldn't let my mother wait too long, or she would be insufferable on the trip back. "I'm sure your life will be easier once I'm gone."

"Perhaps," the demon said. "Or you'll be leaving a mess in your wake."

Chapter
22

Queen Fetia huffed, tugging at her clothes in the privacy of the carriage. Once we were away from the eyes of the demon king's estate, she dropped her pretenses. "How can you stand these clothes? They are cheap and rub against your skin."

I looked out the window, only half listening to her. After days of traveling, I was at my wits' end, and my mind kept wandering back to Ethlow. How many would hate me for leaving them behind without a proper goodbye? Would Reamann ever forgive me? Would he move on with someone else?

I wiped the tears away as covertly as possible, not that my mother was paying attention to me.

"When we get back, you will need to give Prince Sylvar a personal apology for abandoning him a week before your wedding. Maybe he'll want to marry you, even though you're no longer pure. It will fix our relations with the Calamity Sea."

I tightened my fists. It was as if she had already forgotten our deal. Nothing she said would make me marry that prince. I couldn't give myself away like that—not after feeling Reamann's love. More tears poured out. I wanted a life with him. I wanted to wake up with him and see the joy on his face when he ate my cooking. I wanted him to teach me to fight and become stronger.

I wouldn't be allowed to fight as princess and future queen. That was why we had bodyguards. Royalty didn't need to defend themselves when we had others to do it for us. We didn't need to cook, clean, or think for ourselves, because there was always someone else for the job.

"And you won't have to worry about dealing with legs again, since there will be no reason for you to go back to land. I don't know how you dealt with legs for this long. You must truly hate us to give up your fins." She wouldn't stop talking. It was as if she thought she could convince me this was a good idea by talking me into submission.

"Enough!" I snapped, shocking both myself and my mother.

She blinked at me several times before saying, "Excuse me?"

I stared at the crown on her head. It was made of bioluminescent coral. It was beautiful, but it wasn't for me. That life wasn't for me.

I had made the biggest mistake of my life.

"I'm not going to be queen." My chest fluttered as I said those words for the first time. "I don't want this life, mother. You know that, which is why you never bothered to come after me before. I'm sorry Manaia is dead, but I can't replace her. I can't become what she was."

"With time—"

"No," I interrupted. "I'm sorry I was never the daughter you wanted, but I can't do this. Sefina can become queen. Or maybe you and Father can produce another heir. I don't care."

"You can't swim away from this life," she said. "Royalty is in your blood. You were born to be in charge."

"I'm not swimming away from it. I'm walking away from it."

"It's because of that demon, isn't it?" she sneered. "You're throwing your life away for a demon." She would never understand me, even if she tried.

"Even if I was, so what? I didn't want to be part of your plan before him, and I don't want to be part of it now. I love him, and I want to be with him." I poked my head out the window and called out to the carriage driver. "Stop the carriage!"

"If you walk away—"

The horses plodded to a stop, and I opened the door, pausing only to say, "You won't come after me. You won't wage war either. If you do, you'll regret it."

"Love fades," my mother said, her voice laced with ice. "One day you'll wake up and realize choosing him was a mistake."

"I'm not choosing him. I'm choosing me. Goodbye, mother." I jumped out of the carriage and began running down the path back to Ethlow, back to my home.

I stood in front of the large door at the entrance to Ethlow. The first time I stood in front of that door, I was broken and unsure of life. It was my last resort to survive in a world that wasn't the one I had grown up in.

It was different this time. I wasn't running from a life I didn't want. I was running towards a life I wanted. I grabbed the gold ring and knocked three times, taking a shaky breath. The door creaked open, seemingly on its own. I hesitated, unsure if I should step through the entrance.

Viridian stepped out of the shadows and looked me up and down. It had been over a week since I last stepped foot in Ethlow, and I feared I'd be turned away by the master of the house.

"May I help you?" he asked, as if I was a perfect stranger.

"I want to come home." I didn't shy away from his darkened glare. I needed him to understand that I wasn't afraid to come crawling back.

He blinked once, twice. "Do you understand how much trouble you caused me, *Princess*?"

"I know I left without much warning. I thought the responsible thing to do was to go back to my people, but this is where I want to be. This is where I need to be." I was more sure of that than ever before.

Viridian didn't shut the door on my face, which was better than I had expected. "Cibil retired this week, and I suppose I am searching for someone to replace her. Do you think you can handle that responsibility?"

"Yes." There was no hesitation on my end.

"You'll start first thing in the morning. Try your best to not cause any more headaches for me." He stepped to the side, letting me into the estate.

A weight fell off my shoulders as I entered the place that had become my home. There was more I had to face, but the first step was over. I was ready to run to Reamann, despite the ache in my feet from walking for days, but I hesitated, looking back at the master of the house. "You're not going to treat me differently now that you know I'm a princess, are you?"

"I've always known you were a princess." When he saw the shock on my face, he continued, "I know everything about the residents here. I don't let just anyone enter the young sire's estate for his safety and the safety of the other residents. I expect everyone to do their part and follow the rules, no matter their background."

There was something comforting about knowing Viridian had known my secret all along, yet he treated me like everyone else. "Thank you." I walked away, but then his voice stopped me.

"You'll find him in the barracks," Viridian said.

I didn't have to ask who he was talking about. I took off, the need to see Reamann overwhelming. A week away from him was worse than leaving home.

The echo of metal clinking together filled my ears. I stopped running outside the barracks and took a moment to catch my breath. I didn't want Reamann to see how much effort it took me to run. When I stepped inside, Reamann stood in the center of the training area with several beings who weren't trained guards. Among them was Wistari, and her face was covered in sweat.

Reamann gave instructions for basic self-defense, and I watched from the door, not wanting to interrupt the session. I focused on my breathing and what I would say to him. I had thought about a hundred different ways to tell him I was sorry, but none of them felt like enough. I wouldn't have blamed him if he told me he never wanted to see me again.

When he dismissed everyone, Wistari moved up to him and said something to him too quietly for me to hear. Reamann turned around, his eyes immediately landing on me. He stared, frozen like a statue.

The sight of him made it difficult to remember how to breathe. I lifted my hand and said, "Hi." None of my practiced statements came to mind once Reamann's red eyes met mine.

His chest moved up and down, as if he was struggling to breathe. I dropped my hand, afraid of the worst, but then Reamann broke out into a sprint. He wrapped his arms around me and picked me up, spinning me in the air. When my feet found the ground again, he didn't let go, burying his face in my shoulder.

"When I woke up, and you were gone..."

I clung to him, tears streaming down my face. "I'm so sorry." I felt eyes studying us, but I didn't care who was watching.

"Please tell me you aren't leaving again." The desperation in his voice broke me. If the roles had been reversed, it would've left me in shambles.

"I love you too much to leave again."

Reamann pulled back, his cheeks stained with tears. "You love me?"

I opened my mouth to tell him of course I did, but I hadn't said it to his face, despite knowing it. "I love you," I repeated, holding my chin high.

His mouth found mine, and I clung to him, telling myself I would never be stupid enough to leave him again. He was my future and my happiness.

When he pulled back to catch his breath, he stroked my cheek with the back of his hand. "I love you, too."

I bit my bottom lip, trying to hold back the stupid smile that threatened to devour my entire face. "So, you're training people how to defend themselves?"

Reamann glanced over his shoulder at the group who suddenly pretended to be busy to hide the fact that they were staring at us. "Someone I know said everyone should know how to defend themselves."

"She sounds pretty smart," I said.

"Sometimes," Reamann teased. "Sometimes she runs off in the middle of the night and gets herself in trouble." His voice was lighthearted, but we both knew there was real pain behind his words.

"Good thing she's not planning on going anywhere without her trusty demon in shining armor." I looked up, hoping one day I could heal the pain I caused Reamann.

Reamann picked me up, making me squeak. He walked out of the barracks, carrying me back to the house. "She couldn't leave, even if she tried." He squeezed my ass, making me giggle. We would be okay, one piece at a time.

Chapter 23

Satella glared at me with her arms crossed. I thought Reamann would be the hardest one to get forgiveness from, but I had been wrong.

"I made you soup," I said. I made the vampire's favorite soup in hope my bribe would break through her simmering ire.

She pursed her lips, debating about taking my offering. "I do love soup." Her features softened, and I let out a slow breath. "Don't think this means you're off the hook for disappearing for a week without a word."

"I'm sorry," I said, running my fingers through my hair. "I didn't think you'd let me leave."

"We would have supported you, if you had been honest," Nyri said. From what I heard, she had gotten into an argument with Zathrian, since he knew about my mother's request to take me away in the middle of the night and didn't tell her immediately.

"I wouldn't have," Satella said. She grabbed the soup, pulling it closer to her. "I would've told Aukina that she was being stupid by letting her mother manipulate her, and I wouldn't have let her leave."

"Are you ever going to forgive me?" I asked.

Satella took an extra long time to answer, as if that was her version of revenge. "Keep making me soup, and we'll talk."

I chuckled, shaking my head. That was her way of saying yes. I made her soup all the time, so her request wasn't special.

"Okay, enough of this. The others are already waiting for us." Nyri hopped out of her chair and grabbed Satella and me, dragging us out of the mess hall.

"What's so important that I can't finish my soup?" Satella asked.

"You'll see!" Nyri had a skip in her step, and she didn't stop until we were at the greenhouse. Zathrian and Reamann were inside, but no one else was in sight.

Reamann stole me away from Nyri, wrapping his arm around me. Ever since I had come back, he couldn't keep his hands off me—not that I minded. With his request to start a defense training class, his guard shift was changed back to his old schedule, making it easy to spend time with each other.

"This way," Nyri said, holding the demon king's hand. She led us to the back of the greenhouse, which was off limits for regular visitors. A curtain hung in front of the back wall. Nyri stood in front of it, facing the rest of us. "I didn't want to say anything sooner, because I was a little worried it wouldn't work out."

"What wouldn't work out?" Satella asked.

Nyri burst into a wide smile. "This." She pulled the curtain to the side, revealing six buds of bleeding heart lilies. She looked at me directly. "I had already started working on breeding the flower before Ovid stole the one on display. I'm sorry I didn't say anything sooner. I didn't know if they would grow, so I thought it would be a good surprise. And if my calculations are right, I can get them to bloom right here, right now."

I was speechless. There was part of me that had held onto the guilt of leading the merchant to Nyri's prized flower. She hadn't brought it up after, as if her greatest accomplishment getting stolen hadn't mattered. This was why.

"There's so many of them," Satella said.

Nyri let go of Zathrian's hand. "Ready?" When we all echoed a yes, she touched each of the flower's petals, using her magic to feed them life. Then she took a step back.

One by one, the flowers moved, unfurling to reveal the white petals and a blood-red center. When the last flower opened, the white shifted in color, rapidly turning purple. Panic flashed on Nyri's face, and she moved towards the flower, ready to help it.

I held up my hand to stop her. "Wait."

She froze, trusting me as the flower looked like it was going to shrivel. Instead, the white was taken over by a royal purple, and blood-red tendrils turned to streams of gold, flowing from the flower's center.

"I didn't know that was possible," Nyri whispered.

I gently touched the tip of one of the flower petals. "It's a rare variant of the flower," I explained, remembering the tale I had heard on the Nescen Islands. "It's said that the flower changes color in the presence of true love. I always thought it was just a myth, but..." My voice trailed off as I looked at Reamann.

Nyri looked at Zathrian the same way, love burning in her eyes. I didn't know if it was the love Reamann and I shared, or the love of my friend, but seeing the flower shimmer filled my heart to the brim with joy.

"Great. Now I'm the only single one here with you love birds," Satella muttered, but her eyes glowed as she stared at the flower.

"You'll find someone," I said, hopeful for love now that I had it myself.

"Maybe," Satella said, but the smile on her lips was heavy with a sadness I caught on her face from time to time. "But it's okay. I have you guys, and as long as no one else tries to disappear in the middle of the night, I'll be fine." She gave me a pointed look, and this was only the beginning of her comments, but I was okay with that.

With Reamann and my friends at my side, it felt like I was where I truly belonged, and for the first time in a long time, I didn't regret the choices that brought me to Ethlow. I didn't need to be a princess to be happy. I only needed my loved ones at my side to have a bright future.

Author's Note

Thank you so much for taking time to read my book! If you've made it this far, I would greatly appreciate it if you took the time to leave a review on Amazon/Goodreads. As an indie author, reviews are essential for gaining more visibility. All reviews are appreciated! If you ever have any questions, concerns, or general comments, please feel free to reach out to me directly at evereri.theauthor@gmail.com!

ALSO BY EVERERI

Read more in The Demons of Kinzlea

The Demon King's Pet
The Demon King's Cook
The Demon King's Healer
The Demon King's Librarian
The Demon King's Teacher
The Demon King's Assassin

Coming Soon!

The Demon Queen's Rise
Coming in early 2025

The Unfortunate Fate of Mates

Available on the Dreame App:

The Four Beta Brothers
The Stolen Wolf Princess
The Long Lost Luna
The Unwanted Wolf
The Blood Moon Twins

ACKNOWLEDGEMENTS

To my friends who listen to me talk about my books for hours and who have given me brilliant suggestions. To my sister who listens to me about all the good and the bad. You are my loves and my inspiration for this series, and I am grateful to have you all in my life.

For Kelly who *does not* suffer through my raw writing. You push me to write faster to keep up with you.

For Sam for brainstorming with me and answering all my hypothetical questions.

For Amanda for hours spent talking about my struggles and for my writing frog buddy.

For Lauren, my book buddy and our coffee, book, and craft dates.

For Michelle and your thorough reviews of my books that give me a boost of serotonin to push me forward.

ABOUT THE AUTHOR

 EverEri is a lover of romance, fantasy, and fairytales, and one of her favorite things to do is to bring a story and characters alive through the written word. EverEri began her true writing journey in the paranormal romance world in 2021, and she never plans to turn back. Whether it's demons, dragons, werewolves, merfolk, or other magical beings, she plans to bring her passions to life in each book she writes.

Want to see more?

Follow EverEri on social media:

IG: everlastingeri

Tik Tok: author_evereri

FB: EverEri's Reading Group

Newsletter: evereri.theauthor@gmail.com